MERRY TALES

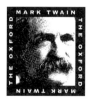

THE OXFORD MARK TWAIN

Shelley Fisher Fishkin, Editor

The Celebrated Jumping Frog of Calaveras County, and Other Sketches
   Introduction: Roy Blount Jr.
   Afterword: Richard Bucci

The Innocents Abroad
   Introduction: Mordecai Richler
   Afterword: David E. E. Sloane

Roughing It
   Introduction: George Plimpton
   Afterword: Henry B. Wonham

The Gilded Age
   Introduction: Ward Just
   Afterword: Gregg Camfield

Sketches, New and Old
   Introduction: Lee Smith
   Afterword: Sherwood Cummings

The Adventures of Tom Sawyer
   Introduction: E. L. Doctorow
   Afterword: Albert E. Stone

A Tramp Abroad
   Introduction: Russell Banks
   Afterword: James S. Leonard

MARK TWAIN

Merry Tales

Mark Twain

FOREWORD

SHELLEY FISHER FISHKIN

INTRODUCTION

ANNE BERNAYS

AFTERWORD

FORREST G. ROBINSON

New York   Oxford

OXFORD UNIVERSITY PRESS

1996

1002196374

OXFORD UNIVERSITY PRESS

Oxford   New York

Athens, Auckland, Bangkok, Bogotá, Bombay

Buenos Aires, Calcutta, Cape Town, Dar es Salaam

Delhi, Florence, Hong Kong, Istanbul, Karachi

Kuala Lumpur, Madras, Madrid, Melbourne

Mexico City, Nairobi, Paris, Singapore

Taipei, Tokyo, Toronto

and associated companies in

Berlin, Ibadan

Copyright © 1996 by

Oxford University Press, Inc.

Introduction © 1996 by Anne Bernays

Afterword © 1996 by Forrest G. Robinson

Text design by Richard Hendel

Composition: David Thorne

Published by

Oxford University Press, Inc.

198 Madison Avenue, New York,

New York 10016

Oxford is a registered trademark of

Oxford University Press

Library of Congress

Cataloging-in-Publication Data

Twain, Mark, 1835–1910.

Merry tales / by Mark Twain ; with an introduction

by Anne Bernays and an afterword by Forrest

Robinson.

p.   cm. — (The Oxford Mark Twain)

Includes bibliographical references.

1. Manners and customs—Fiction. 2. United

States—History—Civil War, 1861–1865—Fiction.

3. Humorous stories, American. 4. War stories,

American. I. Title. II. Series: Twain, Mark,

1835–1910. Works. 1996.

PS1322.M4 1996

813'.4—dc20

96-16577

CIP

ISBN 0-19-510142-1 (trade ed.)

ISBN 0-19-511411-6 (lib. ed.)

ISBN 0-19-509088-8 (trade ed. set)

ISBN 0-19-511345-4 (lib. ed. set)

9 8 7 6 5 4 3 2 1

Printed in the United States of America

on acid-free paper

FRONTISPIECE

Samuel L. Clemens appears here in a full-length

portrait taken around 1888, about four years before

the publication of *Merry Tales*. (The Mark Twain

House, Hartford, Connecticut)

CONTENTS

EDITOR'S NOTE

The Oxford Mark Twain consists of twenty-nine volumes of facsimiles of the first American editions of Mark Twain's works, with an editor's foreword, new introductions, afterwords, notes on the texts, and essays on the illustrations in volumes with artwork. The facsimiles have been reproduced from the originals unaltered, except that blank pages in the front and back of the books have been omitted, and any seriously damaged or missing pages have been replaced by pages from other first editions (as indicated in the notes on the texts).

In the foreword, introduction, afterword, and essays on the illustrations, the titles of Mark Twain's works have been capitalized according to modern conventions, as have the names of characters (except where otherwise indicated). In the case of discrepancies between the title of a short story, essay, or sketch as it appears in the original table of contents and as it appears on its own title page, the title page has been followed. The parenthetical numbers in the introduction, afterwords, and illustration essays are page references to the facsimiles.

Twain often strikes us as more a creature of our time than of his. He appreciated the importance and the complexity of mass tourism and public relations, fields that would come into their own in the twentieth century but were only fledgling enterprises in the nineteenth. He explored the liberating potential of humor and the dynamics of friendship, parenting, and marriage. He narrowed the gap between "popular" and "high" culture, and he meditated on the enigmas of personal and national identity. Indeed, it would be difficult to find an issue on the horizon today that Twain did not touch on somewhere in his work. Heredity versus environment? Animal rights? The boundaries of gender? The place of black voices in the cultural heritage of the United States? Twain was there.

With startling prescience and characteristic grace and wit, he zeroed in on many of the key challenges — political, social, and technological — that would face his country and the world for the next hundred years: the challenge of race relations in a society founded on both chattel slavery and ideals of equality, and the intractable problem of racism in American life; the potential of new technologies to transform our lives in ways that can be both exhilarating and terrifying — as well as unpredictable; the problem of imperialism and the difficulties entailed in getting rid of it. But he never lost sight of the most basic challenge of all: each man or woman's struggle for integrity in the face of the seductions of power, status, and material things.

Mark Twain's unerring sense of the right word and not its second cousin taught people to pay attention when he spoke, in person or in print. He said things that were smart and things that were wise, and he said them incomparably well. He defined the rhythms of our prose and the contours of our moral map. He saw our best and our worst, our extravagant promise and our stunning failures, our comic foibles and our tragic flaws. Throughout the world he is viewed as the most distinctively American of American authors — and as one of the most universal. He is assigned in classrooms in Naples, Riyadh, Belfast, and Beijing, and has been a major influence on twentieth-century writers from Argentina to Nigeria to Japan. The Oxford Mark Twain celebrates the versatility and vitality of this remarkable writer.

The Oxford Mark Twain reproduces the first American editions of Mark Twain's books published during his lifetime.[5] By encountering Twain's works in their original format — typography, layout, order of contents, and illustrations — readers today can come a few steps closer to the literary artifacts that entranced and excited readers when the books first appeared. Twain approved of and to a greater or lesser degree supervised the publication of all of this material.[6] The Mark Twain House in Hartford, Connecticut, generously loaned us its originals.[7] When more than one copy of a first American edition was available, Robert H. Hirst, general editor of the Mark Twain Project, in cooperation with Marianne Curling, curator of the Mark Twain House (and Jeffrey Kaimowitz, head of Rare Books for the Watkinson Library of Trinity College, Hartford, where the Mark Twain House collection is kept), guided our decision about which one to use.[8] As a set, the volumes also contain more than eighty essays commissioned especially for The Oxford Mark Twain, in which distinguished contributors reassess Twain's achievement as a writer and his place in the cultural conversation that he did so much to shape.

Each volume of The Oxford Mark Twain is introduced by a leading American, Canadian, or British writer who responds to Twain — often in a very personal way — as a fellow writer. Novelists, journalists, humorists, columnists, fabulists, poets, playwrights — these writers tell us what Twain taught them and what in his work continues to speak to them. Reading Twain's books, both famous and obscure, they reflect on the genesis of his art and the characteristics of his style, the themes he illuminated, and the aesthetic strategies he pioneered. Individually and collectively their contributions testify to the place Mark Twain holds in the hearts of readers of all kinds and temperaments.

Scholars whose work has shaped our view of Twain in the academy today have written afterwords to each volume, with suggestions for further reading. Their essays give us a sense of what was going on in Twain's life when he wrote the book at hand, and of how that book fits into his career. They explore how each book reflects and refracts contemporary events, and they show Twain responding to literary and social currents of the day, variously accepting, amplifying, modifying, and challenging prevailing paradigms. Sometimes they argue that works previously dismissed as quirky or eccentric departures actually address themes at the heart of Twain's work from the start. And as they bring new perspectives to Twain's composition strategies in familiar texts, several scholars see experiments in form where others saw only form-lessness, method where prior critics saw only madness. In addition to eluci-dating the work's historical and cultural context, the afterwords provide an overview of responses to each book from its first appearance to the present.

Most of Mark Twain's books involved more than Mark Twain's words: unique illustrations. The parodic visual send-ups of "high culture" that Twain himself drew for *A Tramp Abroad*, the sketch of financial manipulator Jay Gould as a greedy and sadistic "Slave Driver" in *A Connecticut Yankee in King Arthur's Court*, and the memorable drawings of Eve in *Eve's Diary* all helped Twain's books to be sold, read, discussed, and preserved. In their es-says for each volume that contains artwork, Beverly R. David and Ray Sapirstein highlight the significance of the sketches, engravings, and pho-tographs in the first American editions of Mark Twain's works, and tell us what is known about the public response to them.

The Oxford Mark Twain invites us to read some relatively neglected works by Twain in the company of some of the most engaging literary figures of our time. Roy Blount Jr., for example, riffs in a deliciously Twain-like manner on "An Item Which the Editor Himself Could Not Understand," which may well rank as one of the least-known pieces Twain ever published. Bobbie Ann Mason celebrates the "mad energy" of Twain's most obscure comic novel, *The American Claimant*, in which the humor "hurtles beyond tall tale into simon-pure absurdity."[9] Garry Wills finds that *Christian Science* "gets us very close to the heart of American culture." Lee Smith reads "Political Economy" as a sharp and funny essay on language. Walter Mosley sees "The Stolen White Elephant," a story "reduced to a series of ridiculous telegrams related by an untrustworthy narrator caught up in an adventure that is as impossible as it is ludicrous," as a stunningly compact and economical satire of a world we still recognize as our own. Anne Bernays returns to "The Private History of a Campaign That Failed" and finds "an antiwar manifesto that is also confession, dramatic monologue, a plea for understanding and absolution, and a romp that gradually turns into atrocity even as we watch." After revisiting Captain Stormfield's heaven, Frederik Pohl finds that there "is no imaginable place more pleasant to spend eternity." Indeed, Pohl writes, "one would almost be willing to die to enter it."

While less familiar works receive fresh attention in The Oxford Mark Twain, new light is cast on the best-known works as well. Judith Martin ("Miss Manners") points out that it is by reading a court etiquette book that Twain's pauper learns how to behave as a proper prince. As important as etiquette may be in the palace, Martin notes, it is even more important in the slums.

> That etiquette is a sorer point with the ruffians in the street than with the proud dignitaries of the prince's court may surprise some readers. As in our own streets, etiquette is always a more volatile subject among those who cannot count on being treated with respect than among those who have the power to command deference.

And taking a fresh look at *Adventures of Huckleberry Finn*, Toni Morrison writes,

> much of the novel's genius lies in its quiescence, the silences that pervade it and give it a porous quality that is by turns brooding and soothing. It lies in . . . the subdued images in which the repetition of a simple word, such as "lonesome," tolls like an evening bell; the moments when nothing is said, when scenes and incidents swell the heart unbearably precisely because unarticulated, and force an act of imagination almost against the will.

Engaging Mark Twain as one writer to another, several contributors to The Oxford Mark Twain offer new insights into the processes by which his books came to be. Russell Banks, for example, reads *A Tramp Abroad* as "an important revision of Twain's incomplete first draft of *Huckleberry Finn*, a second draft, if you will, which in turn made possible the third and final draft." Erica Jong suggests that *1601*, a freewheeling parody of Elizabethan manners and mores, written during the same summer Twain began *Huckleberry Finn*, served as "a warm-up for his creative process" and "primed the pump for other sorts of freedom of expression." And Justin Kaplan suggests that "one of the transcendent figures standing behind and shaping" *Joan of Arc* was Ulysses S. Grant, whose memoirs Twain had recently published, and who, like Joan, had risen unpredictably "from humble and obscure origins" to become a "military genius" endowed with "the gift of command, a natural eloquence, and an equally natural reserve."

As a number of contributors note, Twain was a man ahead of his times. *The Gilded Age* was the first "Washington novel," Ward Just tells us, because "Twain was the first to see the possibilities that had eluded so many others." Commenting on *The Tragedy of Pudd'nhead Wilson,* Sherley Anne Williams observes that "Twain's argument about the power of environment in shaping character runs directly counter to prevailing sentiment where the negro was concerned." Twain's fictional technology, wildly fanciful by the standards of his day, predicts developments we take for granted in ours. DNA cloning, fax machines, and photocopiers are all prefigured, Bobbie Ann Mason tells us, in *The American Claimant.* Cynthia Ozick points out that the "telelectrophonoscope" we meet in "From the 'London Times' of 1904" is suspiciously like what we know as "television." And Malcolm Bradbury suggests that in the "phrenophones" of "Mental Telegraphy" "the Internet was born."

Twain turns out to have been remarkably prescient about political affairs as well. Kurt Vonnegut sees in *A Connecticut Yankee* a chilling foreshadowing (or perhaps a projection from the Civil War) of "all the high-tech atrocities which followed, and which follow still." Cynthia Ozick suggests that "The Man That Corrupted Hadleyburg," along with some of the other pieces collected under that title — many of them written when Twain lived in a Vienna ruled by Karl Lueger, a demagogue Adolf Hitler would later idolize — shoot up moral flares that shed an eerie light on the insidious corruption, prejudice, and hatred that reached bitter fruition under the Third Reich. And Twain's portrait in this book of "the dissolving Austria-Hungary of the 1890s," in Ozick's view, presages not only the Sarajevo that would erupt in 1914 but also "the disintegrated components of the former Yugoslavia" and "the *fin-de-siècle* Sarajevo of our own moment."

Despite their admiration for Twain's ambitious reach and scope, contributors to The Oxford Mark Twain also recognize his limitations. Mordecai Richler, for example, thinks that "the early pages of *Innocents Abroad* suffer from being a tad broad, proffering more burlesque than inspired satire," perhaps because Twain was "trying too hard for knee-slappers." Charles Johnson notes that the Young Man in Twain's philosophical dialogue about free will and determinism (*What Is Man?*) "caves in far too soon," failing to challenge what through late-twentieth-century eyes looks like "pseudoscience" and suspect essentialism in the Old Man's arguments.

Some contributors revisit their first encounters with Twain's works, recalling what surprised or intrigued them. When David Bradley came across "Fenimore Cooper's Literary Offences" in his college library, he "did not at first realize that Twain was being his usual ironic self with all this business about the 'nineteen rules governing literary art in the domain of romantic fiction,' but by the time I figured out there was no such list outside Twain's own head, I had decided that the rules made *sense*. . . . It seemed to me they were a pretty good blueprint for writing — Negro writing included." Sherley Anne Williams remembers that part of what attracted her to *Pudd'nhead Wilson* when she first read it thirty years ago was "that Twain, writing at the end of the nineteenth century, could imagine negroes as characters, albeit white ones, who actually thought for and of themselves, whose actions were the product of their thinking rather than the spontaneous ephemera of physical instincts that stereotype assigned to blacks." Frederik Pohl recalls his first reading of *Huckleberry Finn* as "a watershed event" in his life, the first book he read as a child in which "bad people" ceased to exercise a monopoly on doing "bad things." In *Huckleberry Finn* "some seriously bad things — things like the possession and mistreatment of black slaves, like stealing and lying, even like killing other people in duels — were quite often done by people who not only thought of themselves as exemplarily moral but, by any other standards I knew how to apply, actually *were* admirable citizens." The world that

Tom and Huck lived in, Pohl writes, "was filled with complexities and con-tradictions," and resembled "the world I appeared to be living in myself."

Other contributors explore their more recent encounters with Twain, ex-plaining why they have revised their initial responses to his work. For Toni Morrison, parts of *Huckleberry Finn* that she "once took to be deliberate eva-sions, stumbles even, or a writer's impatience with his or her material," now strike her "as otherwise: as entrances, crevices, gaps, seductive invitations flashing the possibility of meaning. Unarticulated eddies that encourage div-ing into the novel's undertow — the real place where writer captures reader." One such "eddy" is the imprisonment of Jim on the Phelps farm. Instead of dismissing this portion of the book as authorial bungling, as she once did, Morrison now reads it as Twain's commentary on the 1880s, a period that "saw the collapse of civil rights for blacks," a time when "the nation, as well as Tom Sawyer, was deferring Jim's freedom in agonizing play." Morrison be-lieves that Americans in the 1880s were attempting "to bury the combustible issues Twain raised in his novel," and that those who try to kick Huck Finn out of school in the 1990s are doing the same: "The cyclical attempts to re-move the novel from classrooms extend Jim's captivity on into each genera-tion of readers."

Although imitation-Hemingway and imitation-Faulkner writing contests draw hundreds of entries annually, no one has ever tried to mount a faux-Twain competition. Why? Perhaps because Mark Twain's voice is too much a part of who we are and how we speak even today. Roy Blount Jr. suggests that it is impossible, "at least for an American writer, to parody Mark Twain. It would be like doing an impression of your father or mother: he or she is al-ready there in your voice."

Twain's style is examined and celebrated in The Oxford Mark Twain by fellow writers who themselves have struggled with the nuances of words, the structure of sentences, the subtleties of point of view, and the trickiness of opening lines. Bobbie Ann Mason observes, for example, that "Twain loved the sound of words and he knew how to string them by sound, like different shades of one color: 'The earl's barbaric eye,' 'the Usurping Earl,' 'a double-dyed humbug.'" Twain "relied on the punch of plain words" to show writers how to move beyond the "wordy romantic rubbish" so prevalent in nineteenth-century fiction, Mason says; he "was one of the first writers in America to deflower literary language." Lee Smith believes that "American writers have benefited as much from the way Mark Twain opened up the possibilities of first-person narration as we have from his use of vernacular language." (She feels that "the ghost of Mark Twain was hovering someplace in the background" when she decided to write her novel *Oral History* from the standpoint of multiple first-person narrators.) Frederick Busch maintains that "A Dog's Tale" "boasts one of the great opening sentences" of all time: "My father was a St. Bernard, my mother was a collie, but I am a Presbyterian." And Ursula Le Guin marvels at the ingenuity of the following sentence that she encounters in *Extracts from Adam's Diary*.

> . . . This made her sorry for the creatures which live in there, which she calls fish, for she continues to fasten names on to things that don't need them and don't come when they are called by them, which is a matter of no consequence to her, as she is such a numskull anyway; so she got a lot of them out and brought them in last night and put them in my bed to keep warm, but I have noticed them now and then all day, and I don't see that they are any happier there than they were before, only quieter.[10]

Le Guin responds,

> Now, that is a pure Mark-Twain-tour-de-force sentence, covering an immense amount of territory in an effortless, aimless ramble that seems to be heading nowhere in particular and ends up with breathtaking accuracy at the gold mine. Any sensible child would find that funny, perhaps not following all its divagations but delighted by the swing of it, by the word "numskull," by the idea of putting fish in the bed; and as that child grew older and reread it, its reward would only grow; and if that grown-up child had to write an essay on the piece and therefore earnestly studied and pored over this sentence, she would end up in unmitigated admiration of its vocabulary, syntax, pacing, sense, and rhythm, above all the beautiful

timing of the last two words; and she would, and she does, still find it
funny.

The fish surface again in a passage that Gore Vidal calls to our attention, from
Following the Equator: "'The Whites always mean well when they take
human fish out of the ocean and try to make them dry and warm and happy
and comfortable in a chicken coop,' which is how, through civilization, they
did away with many of the original inhabitants. Lack of empathy is a principal
theme in Twain's meditations on race and empire."

Indeed, empathy — and its lack — is a principal theme in virtually all of
Twain's work, as contributors frequently note. Nat Hentoff quotes the following thoughts from Huck in *Tom Sawyer Abroad*:

> I see a bird setting on a dead limb of a high tree, singing with its head tilt-
> ed back and its mouth open, and before I thought I fired, and his song
> stopped and he fell straight down from the limb, all limp like a rag, and I
> run and picked him up and he was dead, and his body was warm in my
> hand, and his head rolled about this way and that, like his neck was broke,
> and there was a little white skin over his eyes, and one little drop of blood
> on the side of his head; and laws! I could n't see nothing more for the tears;
> and I hain't never murdered no creature since that war n't doing me no
> harm, and I ain't going to.[11]

"The Humane Society," Hentoff writes, "has yet to say anything as powerful
— and lasting."

Readers of The Oxford Mark Twain will have the pleasure of revisiting
Twain's Mississippi landmarks alongside Willie Morris, whose own lower
Mississippi Valley boyhood gives him a special sense of connection to Twain.
Morris knows firsthand the mosquitoes described in *Life on the Mississippi* —
so colossal that "two of them could whip a dog" and "four of them could hold
a man down"; in Morris's own hometown they were so large during the flood
season that "local wags said they wore wristwatches." Morris's Yazoo City
and Twain's Hannibal shared a "rough-hewn democracy . . . complicated by
all the visible textures of caste and class, . . . harmless boyhood fun and mis-

chief right along with . . . rank hypocrisies, churchgoing sanctimonies, racial hatred, entrenched and unrepentant greed."

For the West of Mark Twain's *Roughing It*, readers will have George Plimpton as their guide. "What a group these newspapermen were!" Plimpton writes about Twain and his friends Dan De Quille and Joe Goodman in Virginia City, Nevada. "Their roisterous carryings-on bring to mind the kind of frat-house enthusiasm one associates with college humor magazines like the *Harvard Lampoon*." Malcolm Bradbury examines Twain as "a living example of what made the American so different from the European." And Hal Holbrook, who has interpreted Mark Twain on stage for some forty years, describes how Twain "played" during the civil rights movement, during the Vietnam War, during the Gulf War, and in Prague on the eve of the demise of Communism.

Why do we continue to read Mark Twain? What draws us to him? His wit? His compassion? His humor? His bravura? His humility? His understanding of who and what we are in those parts of our being that we rarely open to view? Our sense that he knows we can do better than we do? Our sense that he knows we can't? E. L. Doctorow tells us that children are attracted to *Tom Sawyer* because in this book "the young reader confirms his own hope that no matter how troubled his relations with his elders may be, beneath all their disapproval is their underlying love for him, constant and steadfast." Readers in general, Arthur Miller writes, value Twain's "insights into America's always uncertain moral life and its shifting but everlasting hypocrisies"; we appreciate the fact that he "is not using his alienation from the public illusions of his hour in order to reject the country implicitly as though he could live without it, but manifestly in order to correct it." Perhaps we keep reading Mark Twain because, in Miller's words, he "wrote much more like a father than a son. He doesn't seem to be sitting in class taunting the teacher but standing at the head of it challenging his students to acknowledge their own humanity, that is, their immemorial attraction to the untrue."

Mark Twain entered the public eye at a time when many of his countrymen considered "American culture" an oxymoron; he died four years before a world conflagration that would lead many to question whether the contradiction in terms was not "European civilization" instead. In between he worked in journalism, printing, steamboating, mining, lecturing, publishing, and editing, in virtually every region of the country. He tried his hand at humorous sketches, social satire, historical novels, children's books, poetry, drama, science fiction, mysteries, romance, philosophy, travelogue, memoir, polemic, and several genres no one had ever seen before or has ever seen since. He invented a self-pasting scrapbook, a history game, a vest strap, and a gizmo for keeping bed sheets tucked in; he invested in machines and processes designed to revolutionize typesetting and engraving, and in a food supplement called "Plasmon." Along the way he cheerfully impersonated himself and prior versions of himself for doting publics on five continents while playing out a charming rags-to-riches story followed by a devastating riches-to-rags story followed by yet another great American comeback. He had a long-running real-life engagement in a sumptuous comedy of manners, and then in a real-life tragedy not of his own design: during the last fourteen years of his life almost everyone he ever loved was taken from him by disease and death.

Mark Twain has indelibly shaped our views of who and what the United States is as a nation and of who and what we might become. He understood the nostalgia for a "simpler" past that increased as that past receded — and he saw through the nostalgia to a past that was just as complex as the present. He recognized better than we did ourselves our potential for greatness and our potential for disaster. His fictions brilliantly illuminated the world in which he lived, changing it — and us — in the process. He knew that our feet often danced to tunes that had somehow remained beyond our hearing; with perfect pitch he played them back to us.

My mother read *Tom Sawyer* to me as a bedtime story when I was eleven. I thought Huck and Tom could be a lot of fun, but I dismissed Becky Thatcher as a bore. When I was twelve I invested a nickel at a local garage sale in a book that contained short pieces by Mark Twain. That was where I met Twain's Eve. Now, *that's* more like it, I decided, pleased to meet a female character I could identify *with* instead of against. Eve had spunk. Even if she got a lot wrong, you had to give her credit for trying. "The Man That Corrupted

Hadleyburg" left me giddy with satisfaction: none of my adolescent reveries of getting even with my enemies were half as neat as the plot of the man who got back at that town. "How I Edited an Agricultural Paper" set me off in uncontrollable giggles.

People sometimes told me that I looked like Huck Finn. "It's the freckles," they'd explain—not explaining anything at all. I didn't read *Huckleberry Finn* until junior year in high school in my English class. It was the fall of 1965. I was living in a small town in Connecticut. I expected a sequel to *Tom Sawyer*. So when the teacher handed out the books and announced our assignment, my jaw dropped: "Write a paper on how Mark Twain used irony to attack racism in *Huckleberry Finn*."

The year before, the bodies of three young men who had gone to Mississippi to help blacks register to vote—James Chaney, Andrew Goodman, and Michael Schwerner—had been found in a shallow grave; a group of white segregationists (the county sheriff among them) had been arrested in connection with the murders. America's inner cities were simmering with pent-up rage that began to explode in the summer of 1965, when riots in Watts left thirty-four people dead. None of this made any sense to me. I was confused, angry, certain that there was something missing from the news stories I read each day: the why. Then I met Pap Finn. And the Phelpses.

Pap Finn, Huck tells us, "had been drunk over in town" and "was just all mud." He erupts into a drunken tirade about "a free nigger . . . from Ohio—a mulatter, most as white as a white man," with "the whitest shirt on you ever see, too, and the shiniest hat; and there ain't a man in town that's got as fine clothes as what he had."

> . . . they said he was a p'fessor in a college, and could talk all kinds of languages, and knowed everything. And that ain't the wust. They said he could *vote*, when he was at home. Well, that let me out. Thinks I, what is the country a-coming to? It was 'lection day, and I was just about to go and vote, myself, if I warn't too drunk to get there; but when they told me there was a State in this country where they'd let that nigger vote, I drawed out. I says I'll never vote agin. Them's the very words I said. . . . And to see the

cool way of that nigger — why, he wouldn't a give me the road if I hadn't shoved him out o' the way.[12]

Later on in the novel, when the runaway slave Jim gives up his freedom to nurse a wounded Tom Sawyer, a white doctor testifies to the stunning altruism of his actions. The Phelpses and their neighbors, all fine, upstanding, well-meaning, churchgoing folk,

> agreed that Jim had acted very well, and was deserving to have some notice took of it, and reward. So every one of them promised, right out and hearty, that they wouldn't curse him no more.
>
> Then they come out and locked him up. I hoped they was going to say he could have one or two of the chains took off, because they was rotten heavy, or could have meat and greens with his bread and water, but they didn't think of it.[13]

Why did the behavior of these people tell me more about why Watts burned than anything I had read in the daily paper? And why did a drunk Pap Finn railing against a black college professor from Ohio whose vote was as good as his own tell me more about white anxiety over black political power than anything I had seen on the evening news?

Mark Twain knew that there was nothing, absolutely *nothing*, a black man could do — including selflessly sacrificing his freedom, the only thing of value he had — that would make white society see beyond the color of his skin. And Mark Twain knew that depicting racists with chilling accuracy would expose the viciousness of their world view like nothing else could. It was an insight echoed some eighty years after Mark Twain penned Pap Finn's rantings about the black professor, when Malcolm X famously asked, "Do you know what white racists call black Ph.D.'s?" and answered, "'*Nigger!*'"[14]

Mark Twain taught me things I needed to know. He taught me to understand the raw racism that lay behind what I saw on the evening news. He taught me that the most well-meaning people can be hurtful and myopic. He taught me to recognize the supreme irony of a country founded in freedom that continued to deny freedom to so many of its citizens. Every time I hear of

another effort to kick Huck Finn out of school somewhere, I recall everything
that Mark Twain taught *this* high school junior, and I find myself jumping
into the fray.[15] I remember the black high school student who called CNN
during the phone-in portion of a 1985 debate between Dr. John Wallace, a
black educator spearheading efforts to ban the book, and myself. She accused
Dr. Wallace of insulting her and all black high school students by suggesting
they weren't smart enough to understand Mark Twain's irony. And I recall
the black cameraman on the *CBS Morning News* who came up to me after he
finished shooting another debate between Dr. Wallace and myself. He said he
had never read the book by Mark Twain that we had been arguing about —
but now he really wanted to. One thing that puzzled him, though, was why a
white woman was defending it and a black man was attacking it, because as
far as he could see from what we'd been saying, the book made whites look
pretty bad.

As I came to understand *Huckleberry Finn* and *Pudd'nhead Wilson* as
commentaries on the era now known as the nadir of American race relations,
those books pointed me toward the world recorded in nineteenth-century
black newspapers and periodicals and in fiction by Mark Twain's black con-
temporaries. My investigation of the role black voices and traditions played in
shaping Mark Twain's art helped make me aware of their role in shaping all of
American culture.[16] My research underlined for me the importance of changing the stories we tell about who we are to reflect the realities of what we've
been.[17]

Ever since our encounter in high school English, Mark Twain has shown
me the potential of American literature and American history to illuminate
each other. Rarely have I found a contradiction or complexity we grapple
with as a nation that Mark Twain had not puzzled over as well. He insisted on
taking America seriously. And he insisted on *not* taking America seriously: "I
think that there is but a single specialty with us, only one thing that can be
called by the wide name 'American,'" he once wrote. "That is the national de-
votion to ice-water."[18]

Mark Twain threw back at us our dreams and our denial of those dreams,
our greed, our goodness, our ambition, and our laziness, all rattling around

together in that vast echo chamber of our talk — that sharp, spunky American talk that Mark Twain figured out how to write down without robbing it of its energy and immediacy. Talk shaped by voices that the official arbiters of "culture" deemed of no importance — voices of children, voices of slaves, voices of servants, voices of ordinary people. Mark Twain listened. And he made us listen. To the stories he told us, and to the truths they conveyed. He still has a lot to say that we need to hear.

Mark Twain lives — in our libraries, classrooms, homes, theaters, movie houses, streets, and most of all in our speech. His optimism energizes us, his despair sobers us, and his willingness to keep wrestling with the hilarious and horrendous complexities of it all keeps us coming back for more. As the twenty-first century approaches, may he continue to goad us, chasten us, delight us, berate us, and cause us to erupt in unrestrained laughter in unexpected places.

NOTES

1. Ernest Hemingway, *Green Hills of Africa* (New York: Charles Scribner's Sons, 1935), 22. George Bernard Shaw to Samuel L. Clemens, July 3, 1907, quoted in Albert Bigelow Paine, *Mark Twain: A Biography* (New York: Harper and Brothers, 1912), 3:1398.

2. Allen Carey-Webb, "Racism and *Huckleberry Finn*: Censorship, Dialogue and Change," *English Journal* 82, no. 7 (November 1993):22.

3. See Louis J. Budd, "Impersonators," in J. R. LeMaster and James D. Wilson, eds., *The Mark Twain Encyclopedia* (New York: Garland Publishing Company, 1993), 389-91.

4. See Shelley Fisher Fishkin, "Ripples and Reverberations," part 3 of *Lighting Out for the Territory: Reflections on Mark Twain and American Culture* (New York: Oxford University Press, 1996).

5. There are two exceptions. Twain published chapters from his autobiography in the *North American Review* in 1906 and 1907, but this material was not published in book form in Twain's lifetime; our volume reproduces the material as it appeared in the *North American Review*. The other exception is our final volume, *Mark Twain's Speeches*, which appeared two months after Twain's death in 1910.

An unauthorized handful of copies of *1601* was privately printed by an Alexander Gunn of Cleveland at the instigation of Twain's friend John Hay in 1880. The first American edition authorized by Mark Twain, however, was printed at the United States Military Academy at West Point in 1882; that is the edition reproduced here.

It should further be noted that four volumes — *The Stolen White Elephant and Other Detective Stories, Following the Equator and Anti-imperialist Essays, The Diaries of Adam and Eve,* and *1601, and Is Shakespeare Dead?* — bind together material originally published separately. In each case the first American edition of the material is the version that has been reproduced, always in its entirety. Because Twain constantly recycled and repackaged previously published works in his collections of short pieces, a certain amount of duplication is unavoidable. We have selected volumes with an eye toward keeping this duplication to a minimum.

Even the twenty-nine-volume Oxford Mark Twain has had to leave much out. No edition of Twain can ever claim to be "complete," for the man was too prolix, and the file drawers of both ephemera and as yet unpublished texts are deep.

6. With the possible exception of *Mark Twain's Speeches.* Some scholars suspect Twain knew about this book and may have helped shape it, although no hard evidence to that effect has yet surfaced. Twain's involvement in the production process varied greatly from book to book. For a fuller sense of authorial intention, scholars will continue to rely on the superb definitive editions of Twain's works produced by the Mark Twain Project at the University of California at Berkeley as they become available. Dense with annotation documenting textual emendation and related issues, these editions add immeasurably to our understanding of Mark Twain and the genesis of his works.

7. Except for a few titles that were not in its collection. The American Antiquarian Society in Worcester, Massachusetts, provided the first edition of *King Leopold's Soliloquy*; the Elmer Holmes Bobst Library of New York University furnished the 1906–7 volumes of the *North American Review* in which *Chapters from My Autobiography* first appeared; the Harry Ransom Humanities Research Center at the University of Texas at Austin made their copy of the West Point edition of *1601* available; and the Mark Twain Project provided the first edition of *Extract from Captain Stormfield's Visit to Heaven.*

8. The specific copy photographed for Oxford's facsimile edition is indicated in a note on the text at the end of each volume.

9. All quotations from contemporary writers in this essay are taken from their introductions to the volumes of The Oxford Mark Twain, and the quotations from Mark Twain's works are taken from the texts reproduced in The Oxford Mark Twain.

10. *The Diaries of Adam and Eve,* The Oxford Mark Twain [hereafter OMT] (New York: Oxford University Press, 1996), p. 33.

11. *Tom Sawyer Abroad*, OMT, p. 74.

12. *Adventures of Huckleberry Finn*, OMT, p. 49–50.

13. Ibid., p. 358.

14. Malcolm X, *The Autobiography of Malcolm X*, with the assistance of Alex Haley (New York: Grove Press, 1965), p. 284.

15. I do not mean to minimize the challenge of teaching this difficult novel, a challenge for which all teachers may not feel themselves prepared. Elsewhere I have developed some concrete strategies for approaching the book in the classroom, including teaching it in the context of the history of American race relations and alongside books by black writers. See Shelley Fisher Fishkin, "Teaching *Huckleberry Finn*," in James S. Leonard, ed., *Making Mark Twain Work in the Classroom* (Durham: Duke University Press, forthcoming). See also Shelley Fisher Fishkin, *Was Huck Black? Mark Twain and African-American Voices* (New York: Oxford University Press, 1993), pp. 106–8, and a curriculum kit in preparation at the Mark Twain House in Hartford, containing teaching suggestions from myself, David Bradley, Jocelyn Chadwick-Joshua, James Miller, and David E. E. Sloane.

16. See Fishkin, *Was Huck Black?* See also Fishkin, "Interrogating 'Whiteness,' Complicating 'Blackness': Remapping American Culture," in Henry Wonham, ed., *Criticism and the Color Line: Desegregating American Literary Studies* (New Brunswick: Rutgers UP, 1996, pp. 251–90 and in shortened form in *American Quarterly* 47, no. 3 (September 1995):428–66.

17. I explore the roots of my interest in Mark Twain and race at greater length in an essay entitled "Changing the Story," in Jeffrey Rubin-Dorsky and Shelley Fisher Fishkin, eds., *People of the Book: Thirty Scholars Reflect on Their Jewish Identity* (Madison: U of Wisconsin Press, 1996), pp. 47–63.

18. "What Paul Bourget Thinks of Us," *How to Tell a Story and Other Essays*, OMT, p. 197.

INTRODUCTION

Anne Bernays

It's considered heterodox these days to fret over what an author meant by writing a particular story; intention is deemed to be about as relevant as the brand of laptop used in composition. This makes for a certain hygienic approach to a piece of work, washing away as it does both biographical dead cells and historical scabs. But in the case of "The Private History of a Campaign That Failed," peel off the context and you have thrown away the very thing that gives this short work of semi-fiction its piercing poignancy. Clemens' biographer Justin Kaplan says about "The Private History" that it was, "in a way, an answer to the question of why a former Confederate irregular" should be making money off the greatest Union general of them all — U. S. Grant — by publishing his memoirs. Nothing's simple. We all know that no writer writes anything in a biographical vacuum. The events of a writer's life can't help but pervasively inform every single sentence that takes shape in his or her head; anyone who believes that a writer's life and a work of fiction can be separated like a man and his overcoat has never written a novel. Kaplan goes on to theorize that "the unresolved tensions of [Clemens'] uncomfortable role as a Confederate irregular and deserter" were very much with him when he wrote "The Private History," so much so, in fact, that the story seems to have an awfully long cable on its moral anchor.

"The Private History," the one work in *Merry Tales* that remains with the reader, is a story of lost innocence, a state of mind erased in one soaring leap after the death of a stranger. Clemens' narrative leaves out the usual faltering steps, the relapses and stumbling that make up most educational literature.

The normal maturing process, Clemens implies, is short-circuited in war-time.

Who tells this story? Samuel L. Clemens? Mark Twain, its nominal author? Or someone who could only be the youthful Sam long before he became a writer? Narrator and author come together, swim apart, come together again, become one, become two again. Who is talking?

The literature of retreat has its stars: Tolstoy, Hemingway, Stephen Crane, Tim O'Brien. Retreat is an ideal activity from which to draw conclusions about moral ambiguity. The young Sam Clemens turns tail after one sight of death close up. He never returns, unlike Crane's Henry, who overcomes his cowardice and goes stoically back for more.

Unmatched in the care and handling of *tone*, Clemens has produced in this merry tale about shattered innocence and slaughter an antiwar manifesto that is also confession, dramatic monologue, a plea for understanding and absolution, and a romp that gradually turns into atrocity even as we watch. Like an odor, tone is the characteristic of fiction most difficult to describe. It's a whiff of something being braised in the oil of the writer's imagination. Getting the tone right involves both practiced skill and instinctive artistry. Artistry is about manipulating or, if you prefer a gentler word, seducing the reader — persuading him or her to believe that what you have harvested from your imagination is God's honest truth.

Clemens wrote "The Private History" a couple of months after the publication of *Huckleberry Finn*. Like this novel, it starts out with the narrator appealing directly to "you," as if the two of you were leaning on a bar together, working on a couple of brews. The narrator makes a preemptive strike in the very first sentence, putting himself in a place where you might have put him if he hadn't got there first, and effectively preventing you from asking him if he's really saying he's a coward. So clever. The argument is general: I "started out to do something in [the war] but didn't." "Something" could be anything at all from preparing a meal to shooting at the enemy to collecting corpses. But Sam did nothing.

Before launching the story proper, the narrator dramatizes the quixotic nature of wartime, in which men's allegiance is principally to their own skin. A fellow river pilot, a New Yorker, accuses Sam of disloyalty on the grounds that Sam's father owned some slaves. A little later, the friend changes sides and becomes a Rebel, whereupon he faults Sam for having a father "willing to set slaves free." Six months later, the man has switched sides again and is happily piloting a federal gunboat. "You think I'm rotten," Clemens seems to be saying, "as to that, my erstwhile friend is infinitely worse; he's just another hired gun." This passage, serving as a sort of moral prelude — as though to say, "We are none of us the men you would like us to be, but we do our best in an evil world" — sets the stage for what follows. It also helps get the narrator off the hook with Union veterans and partisans.

We still don't know — will never know — how much of "The Private History" is fact, how much imagination, and how much a blend of the two. In an 1890 letter Clemens writes that he "was a *soldier* two weeks once in the beginning of the war, and was hunted like a rat the whole time," but the details of his soldiering are largely unknown. Because Sam suffers a memory lapse in his account — "We had no first lieutenant; I do not know why; it was long ago" — we are persuaded that it's true; paradoxically, we believe the flawed account more than we would one that seems to be recalled intact. Tim O'Brien has this to say about truth and memory in his novel of the Vietnam War, *The Things They Carried*: "In any war story, but especially a true one, it's difficult to separate what happened from what seemed to happen." O'Brien knows something that both he and Clemens counted on to work for them: the verifiable "facts" of a story are not so crucial as its underlying meaning. "Absolute occurrence is irrelevance," O'Brien writes. "A thing may happen and be a total lie; another thing may happen and be truer than the truth." Real life is in disarray; the fiction writer sorts through the factual elements of her story and, discarding and inventing as she goes, places them in a deliberate, often deceptively simple order. If she does it well she creates a narrative that makes emotional sense, bequeathing to the reader a lingering impression of wonder. The real Samuel Clemens — who in turn covers his identity with the "false" Mark Twain — presents us here with the fictional "I" (the man I call Sam); the real and the fictional flow into each other, much as in *The Things They Carried* the real Tim O'Brien and the fictional protagonist who bears his name are the same man — or are they?

Clemens zooms in for close-ups, introducing his players, lighthearted youths for the most part, who form a "military company" much as boys at any time in any place might form a gang to do a little harmless mischief. The cast of characters, the fifteen members of the Marion Rangers (named for their Missouri county), don't know what they're doing, nor have they any idea what they're getting into. A couple of ranks are doled out: Tom Lyman, a youth without any battle experience, is appointed captain. The narrator is made second lieutenant. Dunlap, who has "some pathetic little nickel-plated aristocratic instincts," is "young, ignorant, good-natured, well-meaning, trivial, full of romance." Reliable? Stalwart? Brave? Disciplined? Where are the soldierly virtues in this man? Poor Dunlap becomes the butt of scarifying humor. It seems he can't stand his name — too common — so he renders it d'Un Lap, which by ingenious semantic juggling he transmutes into Peterson. The others end up calling him Peterson Dunlap. This young man's chief employment thereafter is in naming their camps. A "mongrel child of philology," he is good at it, Sam reports — "no slouch."

Clemens drops hints along the way, drawing over his landscape small gray clouds that will eventually release a torrent, a windstorm of tragedy. These are so fleeting and delicate that it's only after you have read the story once and go back for a second look that you see them for what they are. Combined, they make a strong case that Sam's ultimate shame, his desertion, was the act of a man with the judgment of a child. "We did not think; we were not capable of it." If they had thought about what they were doing, they would have realized that when rangers — soldiers without uniforms — are taken prisoner they are hanged as spies. Yet here is Ed Stevens, "neat as a cat," who views the voluntary formation of the Marion Rangers as a sort of holiday. As for Sam, he's glad not to have to go to work at four every morning, delighted to break the grinding routine of his everyday life. Smith, a "vast donkey" whose nature is mercurial, is both bully and crybaby. In one sentence, Smith is dispatched via the surefooted irony Clemens was so good at: ". . . he had one ultimate credit to his account which some of us hadn't: he stuck to the war, and was killed in battle at last." This is what's called a flash-forward, and although tricky — we don't usually want to know what's going to happen — it has the virtue of focusing the reader's attention. We are beginning to get the idea that this campaign's failure involved more than flying rumors and wet nights.

Next is Jo Bowers, whom Clemens loads down with ten adjectives in one long sentence, among them "huge," "flax-headed," "lazy," "sentimental," "industrious," and "ambitious." Bowers is well liked by his fellows and is appointed "orderly sergeant," while Stevens is made corporal.

This "herd of cattle," self-constituted as a band of irregulars, heads for the town of New London, ten miles away. At first, it's a lark — a group of boys, released from work, out in the fresh air, telling jokes, savoring their freedom from the demands of civilian life. Soon, however, "the steady trudging came to be like work; the play had somehow oozed out of it." The boys grow thoughtful, dispirited, silent. The fun has temporarily run its course.

"According to report" — Sam doesn't indicate its source, it's just a report — five Union soldiers have been spotted near a farmhouse lying directly in their path. Captain Lyman whispers instructions to his men: prepare to attack the house. Any sense of games-playing remaining in the group dissolves on the spot: ". . . we were standing face to face with actual war." It has finally sunk in — you can get killed out there. Lyman's troops refuse to obey. He pleads with them to no avail. They go around the farmhouse instead. This insubordination cheers the men; Lyman goes into a sulk. "Horse-play and laughing began again; the expedition was become a holiday frolic once more." Do all soldiers, trying to baffle their own worst fantasies as they head for the battlefield, laugh and sing? Stephen Crane, in *The Red Badge of Courage*, has the regiment "tramp[ing] to the tune of laughter." The tension slackens yet again as Clemens releases the rope, only to pull it taut a few pages later as the men experience alternating joy and dread.

The Marion Rangers return to their "march." It takes two hours to reach the house of Colonel Ralls, a Mexican War veteran who delivers an old-fashioned pep talk "full of gunpowder and glory" and the sort of "windy declamation which was [once] regarded as eloquence." The colonel gives

Sam a sword worn at the battle of Buena Vista, the most celebrated and spectacular battle of that late war.

Still on their feet, they cover another four miles to some woods near a wide "flowery prairie" half a mile from Mason's farm. Sam says it's "enchanting." The emphasis and reemphasis on the childlike and the illusionary in this "campaign" serve to build up Clemens' justification for his ultimate shameful act. Like his companions, he's callow, mindless, without guile or a healthy respect for real danger, without experience or prescience. They're children, too stupid to realize the stove has been lit and the pot is about to boil over on them.

Soon the men are swimming and fishing in a nearby creek, all thoughts of death and grief at a safe psychic distance; it doesn't take much to dispel the gloom of these battle virgins. Some farmers show up with mules and horses for the Rangers' use "for as long as the war might last"; most everyone believes it will be over in a few months' time. Like the men themselves, these animals are "young and frisky." Clemens idles the narrative while he does a comic turn on Sam's mule, a creature with a habit of "stretching its neck out, laying its ears back, and spreading its jaws till you could see down its works." Other horses get the same sort of hilarious, intricate treatment; this continues for nearly three pages. Clemens, apparently, could not resist interrupting his tale to tell animal stories, one of his most cherished modes.

The Marion Rangers are a band of buffoons governed by chaos. "Nobody," Sam reports, "would cook; it was considered a degradation; so we had no dinner." Finally, everyone pitches in and prepares the meal together. At this point corporal and sergeant start squabbling about which one outranks the other. To settle the argument, Lyman declares their ranks equal, and the men subside.

We don't know how long the Marion Rangers remain in this enchanting place. Intentionally vague, Clemens uses phrases like "by and by" and "every forenoon" to indicate a passage of time. Could be days, could be weeks. This is a dreamlike moment that cannot possibly last. "For a time, life was idly delicious, it was perfect; there was nothing to mar it." The only way to follow perfection is to demolish it, which Clemens does by introducing the "general consternation" aroused by a rumor — again sourceless — that the enemy is closing in on them. All but Captain Lyman opt for retreat, "but he found that if he tried to maintain that attitude he would fare badly, for the command were in no humor to put up with insubordination." Lyman calls for a war council of officers, but the privates, who outnumber them and object to being excluded, do most of the talking and prevail. Now the only question is which direction they should retreat in.

Leaving the horses behind, the men begin their retreat to Mason's farm at night. The way is rocky, hilly. It starts to rain. Mud forms. The men fall, slipping and sliding down a hillside. They complain that "they would die before they would ever go to war again." They lose a keg of gunpowder along with a number of guns. Farmer Mason's dogs grab some of them by the seat of their pants. Candle in hand, Mason comes out onto his porch and invites them into his house, where he peppers them with questions they are unable to answer: "we did not know anything concerning who or what we were running from." Mason makes fun of them. "Marion *Rangers*! good name b'gosh!" he says, and asks why they haven't posted a picket guard or sent out a scouting party. Pretty soon "he made us all feel shabbier than the dogs had done."

A fresh alarm: it seems that a detachment of Union soldiers is heading their way with orders to "capture and hang any bands like ours." The men take off for cover, tramping through mud in wind and rain; the elements of meteorological misery echo their fear of a hanging death. Clemens comes right out with it: "It took the romance all out of the campaign, and turned our dreams of glory into a repulsive nightmare." Reprieve! The alarm turns out to be yet another false one, and without missing a beat, the men revert to their erstwhile lightheartedness; it's as if the alarm had never sounded in the first place.

Abruptly the mood shifts again. More clouds gather as the men, stuck at Mason's farm, where the owners go to bed as soon as it grows dark, become bored and slumberous: "There was nothing to do, nothing to think about; there was no interest in life."

Having taken Mason's ridicule to heart, Captain Lyman orders the posting of a picket — a sentry. The narrator tries to send Sergeant Bowers to do this job. Bowers refuses. Sam can't persuade anyone to do it. They are beginning to develop some common sense, but in wartime this trait is about as useful as a diamond stud. "These camps," writes Clemens, who steps back from the story to generalize about similar militias and repeat his argument, "were composed of young men who had been born and reared to a sturdy independence, and who did not know what it meant to be ordered around by Tom, Dick, and Harry, whom they had known familiarly all their lives, in the village or on the farm." Clemens relates an anecdote he heard from his friend James Redpath. A private tells his citizen colonel, whom he addresses by his first name, that he'd like to go home for a few days to "see how things is comin' on." The colonel says okay but make sure you don't stay away longer than two weeks. The kicker here is that both of them make the correct assumption, namely that the man *will* come back. "This was in the first months of the war, of course," when the ordinary courtesies and gestures of civilian life had not yet given way to those of wartime, when no one is given a leave to see how they're getting on back home and if you're AWOL and they find you, you're in deep trouble.

War — "the grim trade" — must be learned, an education that transforms those men who survive into "machines." There's nothing particularly new in this observation. What makes "The Private History" seem fresh and stunning is Clemens' oblique and ironic approach — starting slow and funny, ending up swift and tragic. His voice is both rueful and darkly comic; the tale specific as a documentary film and simultaneously archetypal, like the Southwestern humor Clemens had absorbed in his marrow since childhood.

Sam finally prevails on Bowers, "by agreeing to exchange ranks with him for the time being and go along and stand the watch with him as his subordinate." The bleakest mode has not yet jelled; everything is still fluid, up for negotiation, friendly, casual, dangerous. The Marion Rangers never do establish a regular nighttime picket, although they manage to post one most mornings. The men sleep in a corncrib swarming with rats who bite their feet.

Although there are almost daily rumors that the enemy is closing in on them, the Rangers have yet to see a Union soldier in the flesh, in spite of having imagined him many times. They find themselves engaged in gallows humor and "forced laughs." Is it beginning to sink in? Is death closer than they think? Clemens sets the scene with a numinous description of the men waiting in the corncrib in the "veiled moonlight." "Presently a muffled sound caught our ears," and a man on horseback appears out of the mist, his figure so indistinct the men can't tell whether or not he's alone. Sam shoves his gun through a crack in the wall. "Somebody" tells him to fire and he pulls the trigger. The man falls off his horse. They wait for his companions. They wait in vain; the rider is alone.

The narrative goes into slow motion. "There was not a sound, not the whisper of a leaf; just perfect stillness; an uncanny kind of stillness." After a while they go out to see what they have done. The man is lying on the ground with his mouth open, gasping for breath. His shirt is soaked with blood. It hits Sam — Clemens says the thought "shot" through him — that he has murdered someone who has never done him any harm. Now he's down on the ground, stroking the dying man's forehead, thinking that he would gladly give over his own life for his victim's. "And all the boys seemed to be feeling in the same way." One death close up is worse than a thousand far off. With the sudden clarity of a fork of lightning illuminating the sky and the landscape beneath it, it strikes Sam that this "thing that I have done does not end with him." This is getting your point across with sublime control, and it is sufficient to blur the moral line between cowardice and pacifism.

The men mourn the dead stranger "as if he had been their brother." Then it turns out that six shots in all were fired at the horseman, so that Sam, in effect, is like a member of a firing squad in which none of the men knows who has the real bullets and who the blanks. Even so, Sam can't get this death off his mind. War, he concludes, is simply the killing of stranger by stranger — men "against whom you feel no personal animosity."

The story could end here. But Clemens apparently feels compelled to explain further: "war was intended for men, and I for a child's nurse." He must have felt a nearly intolerable burden of guilt to bring himself to make this "unmanly" disclosure: I wasn't meant to be a soldier; I am soft like a woman. He tries to lessen the torment of causing an innocent stranger's death by claiming he's a terrible shot, never having hit anything he aimed at. "Yet there was no solace in the thought."

The remaining few pages of the story are a swift wrap-up, skimming the surface. The Marion Rangers fall back to several armed camps, "eating up the country" as they go. By the time they are warned that a Union colonel with an entire regiment is about to sweep over them, they're fed up, they've had it. Half the men, including Sam, quit on the spot. "We had done our share; had killed one man, exterminated one army, such as it was." The Union colonel "whose coming frightened me out of the war" is revealed as the future general of the armies, Ulysses S. Grant.

The final paragraph is addressed not to the familiar "you" but to a loftier audience, namely, "the thoughtful." Again the author pleads for understanding: "it is a not unfair picture of what went on in many and many a militia camp in the first months of the rebellion." "Rabbits" had not yet been turned into the soldiers those who stayed on became. As for Sam, he was not among them. The last sentence is typical Mark Twain, self-mocking, sadly comic, and like the very beginning of the story, deflecting the barb's surprise by sticking himself with it: "I knew more about retreating than the man that invented retreating."

If "The Private History of a Campaign That Failed" is Monticello, then the remaining six tales in this 1892 collection are prefabs by the seashore; they all have an unfinished, rawish texture.

"The Invalid's Story" is an anecdote stretched, like a rubber band, until it almost snaps. The narrator, a bachelor of forty-one who seems "sixty and married," tells a gruesome story whose point could use some sharpening but which manages to keep your attention through its odd and disjunctive humor. Rarely has action proceeded less from character. This is pure plot. Initial situation: on board a train, a box containing guns is switched unwittingly with a box containing a corpse. Additional elements: a package of Limburger cheese, a hideously cold night, and two men, one of them the narrator, shut inside the boxcar along with the guns and the cheese. This is Mark Twain turning backflips one after the other, showing what he can do with material so flimsy you can see through it. The dialogue, of course, is flawless.

"Friend of yourn?"
"Yes," I said with a sigh.
"He's pretty ripe, *ain't* he!"

Clemens does more than most writers could be expected to with this confusion between dead body and smelly cheese — a gag at best. The men try everything from breaking a window to smoking cigars. "No, Cap., it don't modify him worth a cent." They cannot "modify" the situation. Finally, they quit the train. As the narrator's companion puts it, "The Governor wants to travel alone." The narrator, "frozen and insensible," finds that his health is shot. "This is my last trip; I am on my way home to die."

"Luck," a story ten pages long — and these are short pages, containing fewer than two hundred words each — is about the triumph of brainlessness. Again we have a nameless narrator, who chronicles the career of a "renowned" British military hero, Lord Arthur Scoresby, a man dismissed by a clergyman acquaintance of the narrator's as "an absolute fool." "Good, and sweet, and lovable" as a youth, Scoresby was also stupid and ignorant. Nevertheless, he climbs the ladder of academic success through judicious tutoring and lucky cramming. During the Crimean War he commits error upon error, but everyone takes his "idiotic blunders for inspirations of genius." The blunder that secures his permanent fame is a battlefield stratagem resulting from his having mistaken his "right hand for his left." This story suggests that Clemens was blowing off some personal steam, for it's not clear whether he's coming down harder on those the general managed to fool or on the poor man himself.

"The Captain's Story" and "Mrs. McWilliams and the Lightning" are companion pieces to "Luck." Sketches rather than fully realized stories, each serves mainly to expose a specific human imperfection; Clemens hasn't bothered to supply any subtle, dense, rich, or enriching ingredients. The eponymous captain, like the blundering general, is a fool, but here the foolishness is concentrated in the man's overreliance on and misreading of the Bible ("So next morning all the children of Israel and their parents . . .”). Mrs. McWilliams’ defect, explicitly, is her fear of lightning, and implicitly, her addiction to the illogical. “Anybody,” she claims, “that has given this subject any attention knows that to create a draught is to invite the lightning.” In the end the lightning and thunder that have ignited poor Mrs. McWilliams turns out to be the report and flash of cannon set off to celebrate Garfield’s nomination to the presidency.

If only Clemens had let “A Curious Experience” age a little longer, it might have become one of his most interesting stories. The basic situation in this first-person narrative is fertile and provocative: a “ragged lad of fourteen or fifteen” is taken into a Union army garrison by a sympathetic commandant and turns the place upside down. The boy, Robert Wicklow, tells a harrowing personal tale of war, mayhem, and abandonment. The commandant makes him the garrison’s drummer boy. Wicklow is often seen praying and heard singing. “Oh, he just gurgles it out so soft and sweet and low, there in the dark, that it makes you think you are in heaven.” There’s something of Billy Budd in Wicklow, but unlike Melville’s highly concentrated, character-driven narrative, this story goes all over the place for fifty-eight pages, ties and reties itself in knots, teasing the reader with the possibility that Wicklow may be a Rebel spy. Finally, Wicklow is revealed as a fabricator of stories, someone living in “a gorgeous, mysterious, romantic world,” a fabulist whose imaginary life spills dangerously over into his real existence. The main problem with the story is that the “spy” business takes over and the boy’s unnatural journey through a world he cannot comprehend is lost in thickets of melodramatic plot.

The final merry tale in this volume is not a tale at all but a burlesque in the form of a play, “Meisterschaft: In Three Acts,” and an excuse for Clemens to vent his intense — and celebrated — frustration over the eccentricities of the German language. Typically, Clemens converts irritation into satire. This playlet is worth noting only for the amount of comic passion Clemens is able to summon over two women trying desperately to master conversational German, and a watery subplot involving a pair of young lovers. A forgettable character named George ventures that "even German is preferable to death." A second forgettable character says, "Well, I don't know; it's a matter of opinion." George again: "It is n't a matter of opinion either. German *is* preferable to death." A hefty portion of this play is in German, so you have to know the language to get the joke.

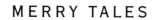

MERRY TALES

MERRY TALES

MARK TWAIN

FICTION FACT

AND

FANCY SERIES

Fiction, Fact, and Fancy Series

Edited by Arthur Stedman

MERRY TALES

MERRY TALES

BY

MARK TWAIN

New York
CHARLES L. WEBSTER & CO.
1892

PRESS OF
JENKINS & McCOWAN,
NEW YORK.

EDITOR'S NOTE.

THE projector of this Series has had in mind the evident desire of our people, largely occupied with material affairs, for reading in a shape adapted to the amount of time at their disposal. Until recently this desire has been satisfied chiefly from foreign sources. Many reprints and translations of the little classics of other literatures than our own have been made, and much good has been done in this way. On the other hand, a great deal of rubbish has been distributed in the same fashion, to the undoubted injury of our popular taste.

Now that a reasonable copyright law allows the publication of the better class of native literature at moderate prices, it has seemed fitting that these volumes should consist mainly of works by American writers. As its title indicates, the " Fiction, Fact, and Fancy Series " will include not only fiction and poetry, but such essays, monographs, and biographical sketches as may appear, from time to time, to be called for.

To no writer can the term " American " more justly be applied than to the humorist whose " Merry Tales " are here presented. It was in an effort to devise some novel method of bringing these stories, new and old, before the public, that this Series had its origin. But, aside from this, those among us who can gather figs of thistles are so few in number as to make their presence eminently desirable.

NEW YORK, March, 1892.

Acknowledgment should be made to the Century Company, and to Messrs. Harper & Brothers, for kind permission to reprint several of these stories from the " Century " and " Harper's Magazine."

CONTENTS.

MERRY TALES.

THE PRIVATE HISTORY OF A CAM-
PAIGN THAT FAILED.

YOU have heard from a great many people who did something in the war; is it not fair and right that you listen a little moment to one who started out to do something in it, but didn't? Thousands entered the war, got just a taste of it, and then stepped out again, permanently. These, by their very numbers, are respectable, and are therefore entitled to a sort of voice,—not a loud one, but a modest one; not a boastful one, but an apologetic one. They ought not to be allowed much space among better people—people who did something—I grant that; but they ought at least to be allowed to state why they didn't do anything, and also to explain the process by which they didn't do anything. Surely this kind of light must have a sort of value.

9

Out West there was a good deal of confusion
in men's minds during the first months of the
great trouble a good deal of unsettledness,
of leaning first this way, then that, then the
other way. It was hard for us to get our
bearings. I call to mind an instance of this.
I was piloting on the Mississippi when the news
came that South Carolina had gone out of the
Union on the 20th of December, 1860. My
pilot-mate was a New Yorker. He was strong
for the Union; so was I. But he would not
listen to me with any patience; my loyalty was
smirched, to his eye, because my father had
owned slaves. I said, in palliation of this dark
fact, that I had heard my father say, some
years before he died, that slavery was a great
wrong, and that he would free the solitary negro he then owned if he could think it right to
give away the property of the family when he
was so straitened in means. My mate retorted
that a mere impulse was nothing—anybody
could pretend to a good impulse; and went on
decrying my Unionism and libeling my ances-
try. A month later the secession atmosphere

had considerably thickened on the Lower Mississippi, and I became a rebel; so did he. We
were together in New Orleans, the 26th of January, when Louisiana went out of the Union.
He did his full share of the rebel shouting, but
was bitterly opposed to letting me do mine.
He said that I came of bad stock—of a father
who had been willing to set slaves free. In the
following summer he was piloting a Federal
gun-boat and shouting for the Union again,
and I was in the Confederate army. I held his
note for some borrowed money. He was one
of the most upright men I ever knew; but he
repudiated that note without hesitation, because I was a rebel, and the son of a man who
owned slaves.

In that summer—of 1861—the first wash of
the wave of war broke upon the shores of Missouri. Our State was invaded by the Union
forces. They took possession of St. Louis, Jef-
ferson Barracks, and some other points. The
Governor, Claib Jackson, issued his proclamation calling out fifty thousand militia to repel
the invader.

I was visiting in the small town where my boyhood had been spent—Hannibal, Marion County. Several of us got together in a secret place by night and formed ourselves into a military company. One Tom Lyman, a young fellow of a good deal of spirit but of no military experience, was made captain; I was made second lieutenant. We had no first lieutenant; I do not know why; it was long ago. There were fifteen of us. By the advice of an innocent connected with the organization, we called ourselves the Marion Rangers. I do not remember that any one found fault with the name. I did not; I thought it sounded quite well. The young fellow who proposed this title was perhaps a fair sample of the kind of stuff we were made of. He was young, ignorant, good-natured, well-meaning, trivial, full of romance, and given to reading chivalric novels and singing forlorn love-ditties. He had some pathetic little nickel-plated aristocratic instincts, and detested his name, which was Dunlap ; detested it, partly because it was nearly as common in that region as Smith,

but mainly because it had a plebeian sound to
his ear. So he tried to ennoble it by writing
it in this way: *d'Unlap*. That contented his
eye, but left his ear unsatisfied, for people gave
the new name the same old pronunciation—
emphasis on the front end of it. He then did
the bravest thing that can be imagined, — a
thing to make one shiver when one remembers how the world is given to resenting shams
and affectations; he began to write his name so:
d'Un Lap. And he waited patiently through
the long storm of mud that was flung at this
work of art, and he had his reward at last; for
he lived to see that name accepted, and the
emphasis put where he wanted it, by people
who had known him all his life, and to whom
the tribe of Dunlaps had been as familiar as
the rain and the sunshine for forty years. So
sure of victory at last is the courage that can
wait. He said he had found, by consulting
some ancient French chronicles, that the name
was rightly and originally written d'Un Lap;
and said that if it were translated into English
it would mean Peterson: *Lap*, Latin or Greek,

he said, for stone or rock, same as the French *pierre*, that is to say, Peter ; *d'*, of or from ; *un*, a or one; hence, d'Un Lap, of or from a stone or a Peter ; that is to say, one who is the son of a stone, the son of a Peter—Peterson. Our militia company were not learned, and the explanation confused them; so they called him Peterson Dunlap. He proved useful to us in his way; he named our camps for us, and he generally struck a name that was " no slouch," as the boys said.

That is one sample of us. Another was Ed Stevens, son of the town jeweler,—trim-built, handsome, graceful, neat as a cat; bright, educated, but given over entirely to fun. There was nothing serious in life to him. As far as he was concerned, this military expedition of ours was simply a holiday. I should say that about half of us looked upon it in the same way; not consciously, perhaps, but unconsciously. We did not think; we were not capable of it. As for myself, I was full of unreasoning joy to be done with turning out of bed at midnight and four in the morning, for a while; grateful

to have a change, new scenes, new occupa-
tions, a new interest. In my thoughts that
was as far as I went; I did not go into
the details; as a rule one doesn't at twenty-
four.

Another sample was Smith, the blacksmith's
apprentice. This vast donkey had some pluck,
of a slow and sluggish nature, but a soft heart;
at one time he would knock a horse down for
some impropriety, and at another he would
get homesick and cry. However, he had one
ultimate credit to his account which some of
us hadn't: he stuck to the war, and was killed
in battle at last.

Jo Bowers, another sample, was a huge,
good-natured, flax-headed lubber; lazy, sentimental, full of harmless brag, a grumbler by
nature; an experienced, industrious, ambitious,
and often quite picturesque liar, and yet not a
successful one, for he had had no intelligent
training, but was allowed to come up just any
way. This life was serious enough to him,
and seldom satisfactory. But he was a good
fellow anyway, and the boys all liked him. He

was made orderly sergeant; Stevens was made corporal.

These samples will answer—and they are quite fair ones. Well, this herd of cattle started for the war. What could you expect of them? They did as well as they knew how, but really what was justly to be expected of them? Nothing, I should say.   That is what they did.

We waited for a dark night, for caution and secrecy were necessary; then, toward midnight, we stole in couples and from various directions to the Griffith place, beyond the town; from that point we set out together on foot. Hannibal lies at the extreme southeastern corner of Marion County, on the Mississippi River; our objective point was the hamlet of New London, ten miles away, in Ralls County.

The first hour was all fun, all idle nonsense and laughter.   But that could not be kept up. The steady trudging came to be like work; the play had somehow oozed out of it; the stillness of the woods and the somberness of the night began to throw a depressing influence over the spirits of the boys, and presently the talking died out and each person shut himself up in his own thoughts. During the last half of the second hour nobody said a word.

Now we approached a log farm-house where, according to report, there was a guard of five Union soldiers. Lyman called a halt; and there, in the deep gloom of the overhanging branches, he began to whisper a plan of assault upon that house, which made the gloom more depressing than it was before. It was a crucial moment; we realized, with a cold suddenness, that here was no jest—we were standing face to face with actual war. We were equal to the occasion. In our response there was no hesitation, no indecision : we said that if Lyman wanted to meddle with those soldiers, he could go ahead and do it; but if he waited for us to follow him, he would wait a long time.

Lyman urged, pleaded, tried to shame us, but it had no effect. Our course was plain, our minds were made up: we would flank the farm-house—go out around. And that is what we did.

We struck into the woods and entered upon

a rough time, stumbling over roots, getting
tangled in vines, and torn by briers. At last
we reached an open plaçe in a safe region, and
sat down, blown and hot, to cool off and nurse
our scratches and bruises. Lyman was annoyed,
but the rest of us were cheerful; we had flank-
ed the farm-house, we had made our first military movement, and it was a success; we had
nothing to fret about, we were feeling just the
other way. Horse-play and laughing began
again; the expedition was become a holiday
frolic once more.

Then we had two more hours of dull trudging and ultimate silence and depression; then,
about dawn, we straggled into New London,
soiled, heel-blistered, fagged with our little
march, and all of us except Stevens in a sour
and raspy humor and privately down on the
war. We stacked our shabby old shot-guns in
Colonel Ralls's barn, and then went in a body
and breakfasted with that veteran of the Mexican War. Afterwards he took us to a distant
meadow, and there in the shade of a tree we
listened to an old-fashioned speech from him,

full of gunpowder and glory, full of that adjec-
tive-piling, mixed metaphor, and windy declamation which was regarded as eloquence in
that ancient time and that remote region; and
then he swore us on the Bible to be faithful to
the State of Missouri and drive all invaders
from her soil, no matter whence they might
come or under what flag they might march.
This mixed us considerably, and we could not
make out just what service we were embarked
in; but Colonel Ralls, the practiced politician
and phrase-juggler, was not similarly in doubt;
he knew quite clearly that he had invested us
in the cause of the Southern Confederacy. He
closed the solemnities by belting around me
the sword which his neighbor, Colonel Brown,
had worn at Buena Vista and Molino del Rey;
and he accompanied this act with another impressive blast.

Then we formed in line of battle and marched
four miles to a shady and pleasant piece of
woods on the border of the far-reaching ex-
panses of a flowery prairie. It was an enchanting region for war—our kind of war.

We pierced the forest about half a mile, and took up a strong position, with some low, rocky, and wooded hills behind us, and a purling, limpid creek in front. Straightway half the command were in swimming, and the other half fishing. The ass with the French name gave this position a romantic title, but it was too long, so the boys shortened and simplified it to Camp Ralls.

We occupied an old maple-sugar camp, whose half-rotted troughs were still propped against the trees. A long corn-crib served for sleeping quarters for the battalion. On our left, half a mile away, was Mason's farm and house; and he was a friend to the cause. Shortly after noon the farmers began to arrive from several directions, with mules and horses for our use, and these they lent us for as long as the war might last, which they judged would be about three months. The animals were of all sizes, all colors, and all breeds. They were mainly young and frisky, and nobody in the command could stay on them long at a time; for we were town boys, and ignorant of horsemanship. The creature that fell to my share was a very small mule, and yet so quick and active that it could throw me without difficulty; and it did this whenever I got on it. Then it would bray—stretching its neck out, laying its ears back, and spreading its jaws till you could see down to its works. It was a disagreeable animal, in every way. If I took it by the bridle and tried to lead it off the grounds, it would sit down and brace back, and no one could budge it. However, I was not entirely destitute of military resources, and I did presently manage to spoil this game; for I had seen many a steamboat aground in my time, and knew a trick or two which even a grounded mule would be obliged to respect. There was a well by the corn-crib; so I substituted thirty fathom of rope for the bridle, and fetched him home with the windlass.

I will anticipate here sufficiently to say that we did learn to ride, after some days' practice, but never well. We could not learn to like our animals; they were not choice ones, and most of them had annoying peculiarities of one kind or another. Stevens's horse would carry him, when he was not noticing, under the huge excrescences which form on the trunks of oak-trees, and wipe him out of the saddle; in this way Stevens got several bad hurts. Sergeant Bowers's horse was very large and tall, with slim, long legs, and looked like a railroad bridge. His size enabled him to reach all about, and as far as he wanted to, with his head; so he was always biting Bowers's legs. On the march, in the sun, Bowers slept a good deal; and as soon as the horse recognized that he was asleep he would reach around and bite him on the leg. His legs were black and blue with bites. This was the only thing that could ever make him swear, but this always did; whenever the horse bit him he always swore, and of course Stevens, who laughed at everything, laughed at this, and would even get into such convulsions over it as to lose his balance and fall off his horse; and then Bowers, already irritated by the pain of the horse-bite, would resent the laughter with hard language, and there would be a quarrel; so that horse made no end of trouble and bad blood in the command.

However, I will get back to where I was —our first afternoon in the sugar-camp. The sugar-troughs came very handy as horse-troughs, and we had plenty of corn to fill them with. I ordered Sergeant Bowers to feed my mule; but he said that if I reckoned he went to war to be dry-nurse to a mule, it wouldn't take me very long to find out my mistake. I believed that this was insubordination, but I was full of uncertainties about everything military, and so I let the thing pass, and went and ordered Smith, the blacksmith's apprentice, to feed the mule; but he merely gave me a large, cold, sarcastic grin, such as an ostensibly seven-year-old horse gives you when you lift his lip and find he is fourteen, and turned his back on me. I then went to the captain, and asked if it was not right and proper and military for me to have an orderly. He said it was, but as there was only one orderly in the corps, it was but right that he himself should have Bowers on his staff. Bowers said he

wouldn't serve on anybody's staff; and if anybody thought he could make him, let him try
it. So, of course, the thing had to be dropped;
there was no other way.

Next, nobody would cook; it was considered a degradation; so we had no dinner.
We lazied the rest of the pleasant afternoon
away, some dozing under the trees, some
smoking cob-pipes and talking sweethearts
and war, some playing games. By late supper-time all hands were famished; and to meet
the difficulty all hands turned to, on an equal
footing, and gathered wood, built fires, and
cooked the meal. Afterward everything was
smooth for a while; then trouble broke out
between the corporal and the sergeant, each
claiming to rank the other. Nobody knew
which was the higher office; so Lyman had to
settle the matter by making the rank of both
officers equal. The commander of an ignorant
crew like that has many troubles and vexations
which probably do not occur in the regular
army at all. However, with the song-singing
and yarn-spinning around the camp-fire, every-

thing presently became serene again; and by and by we raked the corn down level in one end of the crib, and all went to bed on it, tying a horse to the door, so that he would neigh if any one tried to get in.*

We had some horsemanship drill every forenoon; then, afternoons, we rode off here and there in squads a few miles, and visited the farmers' girls, and had a youthful good time, and got an honest good dinner or supper, and then home again to camp, happy and content.

For a time, life was idly delicious, it was perfect; there was nothing to mar it. Then came some farmers with an alarm one day.

---

* It was always my impression that that was what the horse was there for, and I know that it was also the impression of at least one other of the command, for we talked about it at the time, and admired the military ingenuity of the device; but when I was out West three years ago I was told by Mr. A. G. Fuqua, a member of our company, that the horse was his, that the leaving him tied at the door was a matter of mere forgetfulness, and that to attribute it to intelligent invention was to give him quite too much credit. In support of his position, he called my attention to the suggestive fact that the artifice was not employed again. I had not thought of that before.

They said it was rumored that the enemy were advancing in our direction, from over Hyde's prairie. The result was a sharp stir among us, and general consternation. It was a rude awakening from our pleasant trance. The rumor was but a rumor—nothing definite about it; so, in the confusion, we did not know which way to retreat. Lyman was for not retreating at all, in these uncertain circumstances; but he found that if he tried to maintain that attitude he would fare badly, for the command were in no humor to put up with insubordination. So he yielded the point and called a council of war—to consist of himself and the three other officers; but the privates made such a fuss about being left out, that we had to allow them to remain, for they were already present, and doing the most of the talking too. The question was, which way to retreat; but all were so flurried that nobody seemed to have even a guess to offer. Except Lyman. He explained in a few calm words, that inasmuch as the enemy were approaching from over Hyde's prairie, our course was simple: all we had to do was not to retreat *toward* him; any other direction would answer our needs perfectly. Everybody saw in a moment how true this was, and how wise; so Lyman got a great many compliments. It was now decided that we should fall back on Mason's farm.

It was after dark by this time, and as we could not know how soon the enemy might arrive, it did not seem best to try to take the horses and things with us; so we only took the guns and ammunition, and started at once. The route was very rough and hilly and rocky, and presently the night grew very black and rain began to fall; so we had a troublesome time of it, struggling and stumbling along in the dark; and soon some person slipped and fell, and then the next person behind stumbled over him and fell, and so did the rest, one after the other; and then Bowers came with the keg of powder in his arms, whilst the command were all mixed together, arms and legs, on the muddy slope; and so he fell, of course, with the keg, and this started the whole detachment down the hill in a body, and they landed in the brook at the

bottom in a pile, and each that was undermost
pulling the hair and scratching and biting those
that were on top of him; and those that were
being scratched and bitten, scratching and biting the rest in their turn, and all saying they
would die before they would ever go to war
again if they ever got out of this brook this
time, and the invader might rot for all they
cared, and the country along with him—and all
such talk as that, which was dismal to hear and
take part in, in such smothered, low voices, and
such a grisly dark place and so wet, and the
enemy may be coming any moment.

The keg of powder was lost, and the guns
too; so the growling and complaining continued straight along whilst the brigade pawed
around the pasty hillside and slopped around in
the brook hunting for these things; consequently we lost considerable time at this; and
then we heard a sound, and held our breath
and listened, and it seemed to be the enemy
coming, though it could have been a cow, for
it had a cough like a cow; but we did not wait,
but left a couple of guns behind and struck out

for Mason's again as briskly as we could scramble along in the dark.   But we got lost presently among the rugged little ravines, and wasted a deal of time finding the way again, so it was after nine when we reached Mason's stile at last; and then before we could open our mouths to give the countersign, several dogs came bounding over the fence, with great riot and noise, and each of them took a soldier by the slack of his trousers and began to back away with him.   We could not shoot the dogs without endangering the persons they were attached to; so we had to look on, helpless, at what was perhaps the most mortifying spectacle of the civil war.   There was light enough, and to spare, for the Masons had now run out on the porch with candles in their hands.   The old man and his son came and undid the dogs without difficulty, all but Bowers's; but they couldn't undo his dog, they didn't know his combination; he was of the bull kind, and seemed to be set with a Yale time-lock; but they got him loose at last with some scalding water, of which Bowers got his share and re-

turned thanks.   Peterson Dunlap afterwards
made up a fine name for this engagement, and
also for the night march which preceded it, but
both have long ago faded out of my memory.

We now went into the house, and they began to ask us a world of questions, whereby it
presently came out that we did not know anything concerning who or what we were running from; so the old gentleman made himself very frank, and said we were a curious
breed of soldiers, and guessed we could be de-
pended on to end up the war in time, because
no government could stand the expense of the
shoe-leather we should cost it trying to follow
us around.   " Marion *Rangers !* good name,
b'gosh !" said he.   And wanted to know why
we hadn't had a picket-guard at the place where
the road entered the prairie, and why we hadn't
sent out a scouting party to spy out the enemy
and bring us an account of his strength, and so
on, before jumping up and stampeding out of
a strong position upon a mere vague rumor—
and so on, and so forth, till he made us all feel
shabbier than the dogs had done, not half so

enthusiastically welcome. So we went to bed shamed and low-spirited; except Stevens. Soon Stevens began to devise a garment for Bowers which could be made to automatically display his battle-scars to the grateful, or conceal them from the envious, according to his occasions; but Bowers was in no humor for this, so there was a fight, and when it was over Stevens had some battle-scars of his own to think about.

Then we got a little sleep. But after all we had gone through, our activities were not over for the night ; for about two o'clock in the morning we heard a shout of warning from down the lane, accompanied by a chorus from all the dogs, and in a moment everybody was up and flying around to find out what the alarm was about.   The alarmist was a horseman who gave notice that a detachment of Union soldiers was on its way from Hannibal with orders to capture and hang any bands like ours which it could find, and said we had no time to lose. Farmer Mason was in a flurry this time, himself. He hurried us out of the house with

all haste, and sent one of his negroes with us
to show us where to hide ourselves and our
tell-tale guns among the ravines half a mile
away. It was raining heavily.

We struck down the lane, then across some
rocky pasture-land which offered good advan-
tages for stumbling; consequently we were
down in the mud most of the time, and every
time a man went down he blackguarded the
war, and the people that started it, and everybody connected with it, and gave himself the
master dose of all for being so foolish as to go
into it. At last we reached the wooded mouth
of a ravine, and there we huddled ourselves
under the streaming trees, and sent the negro
back home. It was a dismal and heart-breaking
time. We were like to be drowned with the
rain, deafened with the howling wind and the
booming thunder, and blinded by the lightning. It was indeed a wild night. The drench-
ing we were getting was misery enough, but a
deeper misery still was the reflection that the
halter might end us before we were a day older. A death of this shameful sort had not oc-

curred to us as being among the possibilities of war. It took the romance all out of the campaign, and turned our dreams of glory into a repulsive nightmare. As for doubting that so barbarous an order had been given, not one of us did that.

The long night wore itself out at last, and then the negro came to us with the news that the alarm had manifestly been a false one, and that breakfast would soon be ready. Straightway we were light-hearted again, and the world was bright, and life as full of hope and promise as ever—for we were young then. How long ago that was! Twenty - four years.

The mongrel child of philology named the night's refuge Camp Devastation, and no soul objected. The Masons gave us a Missouri country breakfast, in Missourian abundance, and we needed it: hot biscuits; hot "wheat bread" prettily criss-crossed in a lattice pattern on top; hot corn pone; fried chicken; bacon, coffee, eggs, milk, buttermilk, etc.;— and the world may be confidently challenged to furnish the equal to such a breakfast, as it is cooked in the South.

We staid several days at Mason's; and after all these years the memory of the dullness, the stillness and lifelessness of that slumberous farm-house still oppresses my spirit as with a sense of the presence of death and mourning. There was nothing to do, nothing to think about; there was no interest in life. The male part of the household were away in the fields all day, the women were busy and out of our sight; there was no sound but the plaintive wailing of a spinning-wheel, forever moaning out from some distant room,—the most lonesome sound in nature, a sound steeped and sodden with homesickness and the emptiness of life. The family went to bed about dark every night, and as we were not invited to intrude any new customs, we naturally followed theirs. Those nights were a hundred years long to youths accustomed to being up till twelve. We lay awake and miserable till that hour every time, and grew old and decrepit waiting through the still eternities for the clock-strikes. This was no place for town boys. So at last it was with something very like joy that we received news that the enemy were on our track again. With a new birth of the old warrior spirit, we sprang to our places in line of battle and fell back on Camp Ralls.

Captain Lyman had taken a hint from Mason's talk, and he now gave orders that our camp should be guarded against surprise by the posting of pickets. I was ordered to place a picket at the forks of the road in Hyde's prairie. Night shut down black and threatening. I told Sergeant Bowers to go out to that place and stay till midnight; and, just as I was expecting, he said he wouldn't do it. I tried to get others to go, but all refused. Some excused themselves on account of the weather; but the rest were frank enough to say they wouldn't go in any kind of weather. This kind of thing sounds odd now, and impossible, but there was no surprise in it at the time. On the contrary, it seemed a perfectly natural thing to do. There were scores of little camps scattered over Missouri where the same thing

was happening.   These camps were composed
of young men who had been born and reared
to a sturdy independence, and who did not
know what it meant to be ordered around by
Tom, Dick, and Harry, whom they had known
familiarly all their lives, in the village or on the
farm.   It is quite within the probabilities that
this same thing was happening all over the
South.   James Redpath recognized the justice
of this assumption, and furnished the following
instance in support of it.   During a short stay
in East Tennessee he was in a citizen colonel's
tent one day, talking, when a big private appeared at the door, and without salute or other
circumlocution said to the colonel,—

   " Say, Jim, I'm a-goin' home for a few days."
   " What for ? "
   " Well, I hain't b'en there for a right smart
while, and I'd like to see how things is comin'
on."
   " How long are you going to be gone ? "
   " 'Bout two weeks."
   " Well, don't be gone longer than that; and
get back sooner if you can."

That was all, and the citizen officer resumed his conversation where the private had broken it off. This was in the first months of the war, of course. The camps in our part of Missouri were under Brigadier-General Thomas H. Harris. He was a townsman of ours, a first-rate fellow, and well liked; but we had all familiarly known him as the sole and modest-salaried operator in our telegraph office, where he had to send about one dispatch a week in ordinary times, and two when there was a rush of business; consequently, when he appeared in our midst one day, on the wing, and delivered a military command of some sort, in a large military fashion, nobody was surprised at the response which he got from the assembled soldiery,—

"Oh, now, what'll you take to *don't*, Tom Harris!"

It was quite the natural thing. One might justly imagine that we were hopeless material for war. And so we seemed, in our ignorant state; but there were those among us who afterward learned the grim trade; learned to obey like machines; became valuable soldiers; fought all through the war, and came out at the end with excellent records. One of the very boys who refused to go out on picket duty that night, and called me an ass for thinking he would expose himself to danger in such a foolhardy way, had become distinguished for intrepidity before he was a year older.

I did secure my picket that night—not by authority, but by diplomacy. I got Bowers to go, by agreeing to exchange ranks with him for the time being, and go along and stand the watch with him as his subordinate. We staid out there a couple of dreary hours in the pitchy darkness and the rain, with nothing to modify the dreariness but Bowers's monotonous growlings at the war and the weather; then we began to nod, and presently found it next to impossible to stay in the saddle; so we gave up the tedious job, and went back to the camp without waiting for the relief guard. We rode into camp without interruption or objection from anybody, and the enemy could have done the same, for there were no sentries.

Everybody was asleep; at midnight there was nobody to send out another picket, so none was sent. We never tried to establish a watch at night again, as far as I remember, but we generally kept a picket out in the daytime.

In that camp the whole command slept on the corn in the big corn-crib; and there was usually a general row before morning, for the place was full of rats, and they would scramble over the boys' bodies and faces, annoying and irritating everybody; and now and then they would bite some one's toe, and the person who owned the toe would start up and magnify his English and begin to throw corn in the dark. The ears were half as heavy as bricks, and when they struck they hurt. The persons struck would respond, and inside of five minutes every man would be locked in a death-grip with his neighbor. There was a grievous deal of blood shed in the corn-crib, but this was all that was spilt while I was in the war. No, that is not quite true. But for one circumstance it would have been all. I will come to that now.

Our scares were frequent. Every few days rumors would come that the enemy were approaching. In these cases we always fell back on some other camp of ours; we never staid where we were. But the rumors always turned out to be false; so at last even we began to grow indifferent to them. One night a negro was sent to our corn-crib with the same old warning : the enemy was hovering in our neighborhood. We all said let him hover. We resolved to stay still and be comfortable. It was a fine warlike resolution, and no doubt we all felt the stir of it in our veins—for a moment. We had been having a very jolly time, that was full of horse-play and school-boy hilarity; but that cooled down now, and presently the fast-waning fire of forced jokes and forced laughs died out altogether, and the company became silent. Silent and nervous. And soon uneasy — worried — apprehensive. We had said we would stay, and we were committed. We could have been persuaded to go, but there was nobody brave enough to suggest it. An almost noiseless movement presently began in the dark, by a general but un-voiced impulse. When the movement was completed, each man knew that he was not the only person who had crept to the front wall and had his eye at a crack between the logs. No, we were all there; all there with our hearts in our throats, and staring out toward the sugar-troughs where the forest foot-path came through. It was late, and was a deep woodsy stillness everywhere. There was a veiled moonlight, which was only just strong enough to enable us to mark the general shape of objects. Presently a muffled sound caught our ears, and we recognized it as the hoof-beats of a horse or horses. And right away a figure appeared in the forest path; it could have been made of smoke, its mass had so little sharpness of outline. It was a man on horseback; and it seemed to me that there were others behind him. I got hold of a gun in the dark, and pushed it through a crack between the logs, hardly knowing what I was doing, I was so dazed with fright. Somebody said "Fire!" I pulled the trigger. I seemed to see a hundred flashes and hear a hundred reports, then I saw the man fall down out of the saddle. My first feeling was of surprised gratification; my first impulse was an apprentice-sportsman's impulse to run and pick up his game. Somebody said, hardly audibly, "Good—we've got him! — wait for the rest." But the rest did not come. We waited — listened—still no more came. There was not a sound, not the whisper of a leaf; just perfect stillness; an uncanny kind of stillness, which was all the more uncanny on account of the damp, earthy, late-night smells now rising and pervading it. Then, wondering, we crept stealthily out, and approached the man. When we got to him the moon revealed him distinctly. He was lying on his back, with his arms abroad; his mouth was open and his chest heaving with long gasps, and his white shirt-front was all splashed with blood. The thought shot through me that I was a murderer; that I had killed a man—a man who had never done me any harm. That was the coldest sensation that ever went through my marrow. I was down by him in a moment, helplessly stroking his forehead; and I would have given anything then—my own life freely —to make him again what he had been five minutes before. And all the boys seemed to be feeling in the same way; they hung over him, full of pitying interest, and tried all they could to help him, and said all sorts of regretful things. They had forgotten all about the enemy ; they thought only of this one forlorn unit of the foe. Once my imagination persuaded me that the dying man gave me a reproachful look out of his shadowy eyes, and it seemed to me that I could rather he had stabbed me than done that. He muttered and mumbled like a dreamer in his sleep, about his wife and his child; and I thought with a new despair, "This thing that I have done does not end with him; it falls upon *them* too, and they never did me any harm, any more than he."

In a little while the man was dead. He was killed in war; killed in fair and legitimate war; killed in battle, as you may say; and yet he

was as sincerely mourned by the opposing
force as if he had been their brother. The
boys stood there a half hour sorrowing over
him, and recalling the details of the tragedy,
and wondering who he might be, and if he
were a spy, and saying that if it were to do
over again they would not hurt him unless he
attacked them first. It soon came out that
mine was not the only shot fired; there were
five others,—a division of the guilt which was
a grateful relief to me, since it in some degree
lightened and diminished the burden I was
carrying. There were six shots fired at once;
but I was not in my right mind at the time,
and my heated imagination had magnified my
one shot into a volley.

The man was not in uniform, and was not
armed. He was a stranger in the country;
that was all we ever found out about him.
The thought of him got to preying upon me
every night; I could not get rid of it. I could
not drive it away, the taking of that unoffend-
ing life seemed such a wanton thing. And it
seemed an epitome of war; that all war must

be just that—the killing of strangers against whom you feel no personal animosity; strangers whom, in other circumstances, you would help if you found them in trouble, and who would help you if you needed it. My campaign was spoiled. It seemed to me that I was not rightly equipped for this awful business; that war was intended for men, and I for a child's nurse. I resolved to retire from this avocation of sham soldiership while I could save some remnant of my self-respect. These morbid thoughts clung to me against reason; for at bottom I did not believe I had touched that man. The law of probabilities decreed me guiltless of his blood; for in all my small experience with guns I had never hit anything I had tried to hit, and I knew I had done my best to hit him. Yet there was no solace in the thought. Against a diseased imagination, demonstration goes for nothing.

The rest of my war experience was of a piece with what I have already told of it. We kept monotonously falling back upon one camp or another, and eating up the country.

I marvel now at the patience of the farmers
and their families. They ought to have shot
us; on the contrary, they were as hospitably
kind and courteous to us as if we had de-
served it. In one of these camps we found Ab
Grimes, an Upper Mississippi pilot, who afterwards became famous as a dare-devil rebel
spy, whose career bristled with desperate adventures. The look and style of his comrades
suggested that they had not come into the war
to play, and their deeds made good the con-
jecture later. They were fine horsemen and
good revolver-shots ; but their favorite arm
was the lasso. Each had one at his pommel,
and could snatch a man out of the saddle with
it every time, on a full gallop, at any reasonable distance.

In another camp the chief was a fierce and
profane old blacksmith of sixty, and he had
furnished his twenty recruits with gigantic
home-made bowie-knives, to be swung with
the two hands, like the *machetes* of the Isth-
mus. It was a grisly spectacle to see that
earnest band practicing their murderous cuts

and slashes under the eye of that remorseless old fanatic.

The last camp which we fell back upon was in a hollow near the village of Florida, where I was born — in Monroe County.   Here we were warned, one day, that a Union colonel was sweeping down on us with a whole regiment at his heels.   This looked decidedly serious.   Our boys went apart and consulted; then we went back and told the other companies present that the war was a disappointment to us and we were going to disband. They were getting ready, themselves, to fall back on some place or other, and were only waiting for General Tom Harris, who was expected to arrive at any moment; so they tried to persuade us to wait a little while, but the majority of us said no, we were accustomed to falling back, and didn't need any of Tom Harris's help; we could get along perfectly well without him—and save time too.   So about half of our fifteen, including myself, mounted and left on the instant; the others yielded to persuasion and staid—staid through the war.

An hour later we met General Harris on the road, with two or three people in his company —his staff, probably, but we could not tell; none of them were in uniform; uniforms had not come into vogue among us yet. Harris ordered us back; but we told him there was a Union colonel coming with a whole regiment in his wake, and it looked as if there was going to be a disturbance; so we had concluded to go home. He raged a little, but it was of no use; our minds were made up. We had done our share; had killed one man, exterminated one army, such as it was; let him go and kill the rest, and that would end the war. I did not see that brisk young general again until last year; then he was wearing white hair and whiskers.

In time I came to know that Union colonel whose coming frightened me out of the war and crippled the Southern cause to that extent —General Grant. I came within a few hours of seeing him when he was as unknown as I was myself; at a time when anybody could have said, "Grant?—Ulysses S. Grant? I do not remember hearing the name before." It seems difficult to realize that there was once a time when such a remark could be rationally made; but there *was*, and I was within a few miles of the place and the occasion too, though proceeding in the other direction.

The thoughtful will not throw this war-paper of mine lightly aside as being valueless. It has this value: it is a not unfair picture of what went on in many and many a militia camp in the first months of the rebellion, when the green recruits were without discipline, without the steadying and heartening influence of trained leaders; when all their circumstances were new and strange, and charged with exaggerated terrors, and before the invaluable experience of actual collision in the field had turned them from rabbits into soldiers. If this side of the picture of that early day has not before been put into history, then history has been to that degree incomplete, for it had and has its rightful place there. There was more Bull Run material scattered through the early camps of this country than exhibited itself at Bull Run. And yet it learned its trade presently, and helped to fight the great battles later. I could have become a soldier myself, if I had waited. I had got part of it learned; I knew more about retreating than the man that invented retreating.

THE INVALID'S STORY.

I SEEM sixty and married, but these effects are due to my condition and sufferings, for I am a bachelor, and only forty-one. It will be hard for you to believe that I, who am now but a shadow, was a hale, hearty man two short years ago,—a man of iron, a very athlete! —yet such is the simple truth. But stranger still than this fact is the way in which I lost my health. I lost it through helping to take care of a box of guns on a two-hundred-mile railway journey one winter's night. It is the actual truth, and I will tell you about it.

I belong in Cleveland, Ohio. One winter's night, two years ago, I reached home just after dark, in a driving snow-storm, and the first thing I heard when I entered the house was that my dearest boyhood friend and school-mate, John B. Hackett, had died the day be-fore, and that his last utterance had been a desire that I would take his remains home to his poor old father and mother in Wisconsin. I was greatly shocked and grieved, but there was no time to waste in emotions; I must start at once. I took the card, marked " Deacon Levi Hackett, Bethlehem, Wisconsin," and hurried off through the whistling storm to the railway station.   Arrived there I found the long white-pine box which had been described to me; I fastened the card to it with some tacks, saw it put safely aboard the express car, and then ran into the eating-room to provide myself with a sandwich and some cigars. When I returned, presently, there was my coffin-box *back again*, apparently, and a young fellow examining around it, with a card in his hand, and some tacks and a hammer!   I was astonished and puzzled.   He began to nail on his card, and I rushed out to the express car, in a good deal of a state of mind, to ask for an explanation.   But no—there was my box, all right, in the express car; it hadn't been disturbed.   [The fact is that without my suspecting it a prodigious mistake had been made.   I was carrying off a box of *guns* which that young fellow had come to the station to ship to a rifle company in Peoria, Illinois, and *he* had got my corpse!] Just then the conductor sung out " All aboard," and I jumped into the express car and got a comfortable seat on a bale of buckets. The expressman was there, hard at work,—a plain man of fifty, with a simple, honest, good - natured face, and a breezy, practical heartiness in his general style. As the train moved off a stranger skipped into the car and set a package of peculiarly mature and capable Limburger cheese on one end of my coffin-box—I mean my box of guns. That is to say, I know *now* that it was Limburger cheese, but at that time I never had heard of the article in my life, and of course was wholly ignorant of its character. Well, we sped through the wild night, the bitter storm raged on, a cheerless misery stole over me, my heart went down, down, down! The old express-man made a brisk remark or two about the tempest and the arctic weather, slammed his sliding doors to, and bolted them, closed his

window down tight, and then went bustling
around, here and there and yonder, setting
things to rights, and all the time contentedly
humming "Sweet By and By," in a low tone,
and flatting a good deal. Presently I began
to detect a most evil and searching odor stealing about on the frozen air.   This depressed my
spirits still more, because of course I attribut-
ed it to my poor departed friend.   There was
something infinitely saddening about his calling himself to my remembrance in this dumb
pathetic way, so it was hard to keep the tears
back.   Moreover, it distressed me on account
of the old expressman, who, I was afraid,
might notice it.   However, he went humming
tranquilly on, and gave no sign; and for this
I was grateful.   Grateful, yes, but still uneasy;
and soon I began to feel more and more uneasy every minute, for every minute that went
by that odor thickened up the more, and got to
be more and more gamey and hard to stand.
Presently, having got things arranged to his
satisfaction, the expressman got some wood
and made up a tremendous fire in his stove.

This distressed me more than I can tell, for I could not but feel that it was a mistake. I was sure that the effect would be deleterious upon my poor departed friend. Thompson — the expressman's name was Thompson, as I found out in the course of the night—now went poking around his car, stopping up whatever stray cracks he could find, remarking that it didn't make any difference what kind of a night it was outside, he calculated to make *us* comfortable, anyway. I said nothing, but I believed he was not choosing the right way. Meantime he was humming to himself just as before; and meantime, too, the stove was getting hotter and hotter, and the place closer and closer. I felt myself growing pale and qualmish, but grieved in silence and said nothing. Soon I noticed that the " Sweet By and By" was gradually fading out; next it ceased altogether, and there was an ominous stillness. After a few moments Thompson said,—

" Pfew ! I reckon it ain't no cinnamon 't I've loaded up thish-yer stove with ! "

He gasped once or twice, then moved toward

the cof—gun-box, stood over that Limburger cheese part of a moment, then came back and sat down near me, looking a good deal impressed. After a contemplative pause, he said, indicating the box with a gesture,—

" Friend of yourn ? "

" Yes," I said with a sigh.

" He's pretty ripe, *ain't* he ! "

Nothing further was said for perhaps a couple of minutes, each being busy with his own thoughts ; then Thompson said, in a low, awed voice,—

"Sometimes it's uncertain whether they're really gone or not,—*seem* gone, you know—body warm, joints limber—and so, although you *think* they're gone, you don't really know. I've had cases in my car. It's perfectly awful, becuz *you* don't know what minute they'll rise up and look at you ! " Then, after a pause, and slightly lifting his elbow toward the box,— " But *he* ain't in no trance ! No, sir, I go bail for *him !* "

We sat some time, in meditative silence, listening to the wind and the roar of the train;

then Thompson said, with a good deal of feeling,—

"Well-a-well, we've all got to go, they ain't no getting around it. Man that is born of woman is of few days and far between, as Scriptur' says. Yes, you look at it any way you want to, it's awful solemn and cur'us: they ain't *nobody* can get around it ; *all's* got to go —just *everybody*, as you may say. One day you're hearty and strong"—here he scrambled to his feet and broke a pane and stretched his nose out at it a moment or two, then sat down again while I struggled up and thrust my nose out at the same place, and this we kept on doing every now and then—"and next day he's cut down like the grass, and the places which knowed him then knows him no more forever, as Scriptur' says. Yes'ndeedy, it's awful solemn and cur'us ; but we've all got to go, one time or another; they ain't no getting around it."

There was another long pause ; then,—

"What did he die of ?"

I said I didn't know.

" How long has he ben dead ? "

It seemed judicious to enlarge the facts to fit the probabilities ; so I said,—

" Two or three days."

But it did no good; for Thompson received it with an injured look which plainly said, " Two or three *years*, you mean."   Then he went right along, placidly ignoring my state-ment, and gave his views at considerable length upon the unwisdom of putting off bur-ials too long.   Then he lounged off toward the box, stood a moment, then came back on a sharp trot and visited the broken pane, observ-ing,—

" 'Twould 'a' ben a dum sight better, all around, if they'd started him along last sum-mer."

Thompson sat down and buried his face in his red silk handkerchief, and began to slowly sway and rock his body like one who is doing his best to endure the almost unendurable. By this time the fragrance—if you may call it fra-grance—was just about suffocating, as near as you can come at it. Thompson's face was turning gray; I knew mine hadn't any color left in it. By and by Thompson rested his forehead in his left hand, with his elbow on his knee, and sort of waved his red handkerchief towards the box with his other hand, and said,—

"I've carried a many a one of 'em,—some of 'em considerable overdue, too,—but, lordy, he just lays over 'em all!—and does it *easy*. Cap., they was heliotrope to *him !*"

This recognition of my poor friend gratified me, in spite of the sad circumstances, because it had so much the sound of a compliment.

Pretty soon it was plain that something had got to be done. I suggested cigars. Thompson thought it was a good idea. He said,—

"Likely it'll modify him some."

We puffed gingerly along for a while, and tried hard to imagine that things were improved. But it wasn't any use. Before very long, and without any consultation, both cigars were quietly dropped from our nerveless fingers at the same moment. Thompson said, with a sigh,—

"No, Cap., it don't modify him worth a cent.

Fact is, it makes him worse, becuz it appears
to stir up his ambition.   What do you reckon
we better do, now?"

I was not able to suggest anything; indeed,
I had to be swallowing and swallowing, all the
time, and did not like to trust myself to speak.
Thompson fell to maundering, in a desultory
and low-spirited way, about the miserable experiences of this night; and he got to referring
to my poor friend by various titles,—sometimes military ones, sometimes civil ones; and
I noticed that as fast as my poor friend's
effectiveness grew, Thompson promoted him
accordingly,—gave him a bigger title.   Finally
he said,—

"I've got an idea.   Suppos'n we buckle
down to it and give the Colonel a bit of a shove
towards t'other end of the car?—about ten foot,
say.   He wouldn't have so much influence,
then, don't you reckon?"

I said it was a good scheme.   So we took in
a good fresh breath at the broken pane, calcu-
lating to hold it till we got through; then we
went there and bent over that deadly cheese

and took a grip on the box. Thompson nod-
ded " All ready," and then we threw ourselves
forward with all our might; but Thompson
slipped, and slumped down with his nose on
the cheese, and his breath got loose. He
gagged and gasped, and floundered up and
made a break for the door, pawing the air and
saying, hoarsely, " Don't hender me !—gimme
the road ! I'm a-dying; gimme the road ! "
Out on the cold platform I sat down and held
his head a while, and he revived. Presently he
said,—

" Do you reckon we started the Gen'rul
any ? "

I said no; we hadn't budged him.

" Well, then, *that* idea's up the flume. We
got to think up something else. He's suited
wher' he is, I reckon ; and if that's the way he
feels about it, and has made up his mind that
he don't wish to be disturbed, you bet he's
a-going to have his own way in the business.
Yes, better leave him right wher' he is, long as
he wants it so ; becuz he holds all the trumps,
don't you know, and so it stands to reason

that the man that lays out to alter his plans for him is going to get left."

But we couldn't stay out there in that mad storm ; we should have frozen to death.   So we went in again and shut the door, and began to suffer once more and take turns at the break in the window.   By and by, as we were starting away from a station where we had stopped a moment Thompson pranced in cheerily, and exclaimed,—

" We're all right, now !   I reckon we've got the Commodore this time.   I judge I've got the stuff here that'll take the tuck out of him."

It was carbolic acid.   He had a carboy of it. He sprinkled it all around everywhere ; in fact he drenched everything with it, rifle-box, cheese and all.   Then we sat down, feeling pretty hopeful.   But it wasn't for long.   You see the two perfumes began to mix, and then —well, pretty soon we made a break for the door ; and out there Thompson swabbed his face with his bandanna and said in a kind of disheartened way,—

" It ain't no use.   We can't buck agin *him*.

He just utilizes everything we put up to modify
him with, and gives it his own flavor and plays
it back on us. Why, Cap., don't you know, it's
as much as a hundred times worse in there now
than it was when he first got a-going. I never
did see one of 'em warm up to his work so, and
take such a dumnation interest in it. No, sir,
I never did, as long as I've ben on the road;
and I've carried a many a one of 'em, as I was
telling you."

We went in again, after we were frozen
pretty stiff; but my, we couldn't *stay* in, now.
So we just waltzed back and forth, freezing,
and thawing, and stifling, by turns. In about
an hour we stopped at another station; and as
we left it Thompson came in with a bag, and
said,—

"Cap., I'm a-going to chance him once
more,—just this once; and if we don't fetch him
this time, the thing for us to do, is to just throw
up the sponge and withdraw from the canvass.
That's the way *I* put it up."

He had brought a lot of chicken feathers,
and dried apples, and leaf tobacco, and rags,

and old shoes, and sulphur, and assafœtida, and one thing or another ; and he piled them on a breadth of sheet iron in the middle of the floor, and set fire to them. When they got well started, I couldn't see, myself, how even the corpse could stand it. All that went before was just simply poetry to that smell,—but mind you, the original smell stood up out of it just as sublime as ever,—fact is, these other smells just seemed to give it a better hold ; and my, how rich it was ! I didn't make these reflections there — there wasn't time — made them on the platform. And breaking for the platform, Thompson got suffocated and fell ; and before I got him dragged out, which I did by the collar, I was mighty near gone myself. When we revived, Thompson said deject-edly,—

" We got to stay out here, Cap. We got to do it. They ain't no other way. The Governor wants to travel alone, and he's fixed so he can outvote us."

And presently he added,—

" And don't you know, we're *pisoned*. It's

our last trip, you can make up your mind to it. Typhoid fever is what's going to come of this. I feel it a-coming right now. Yes, sir, we're elected, just as sure as you're born."

We were taken from the platform an hour later, frozen and insensible, at the next station, and I went straight off into a virulent fever, and never knew anything again for three weeks. I found out, then, that I had spent that awful night with a harmless box of rifles and a lot of innocent cheese; but the news was too late to save *me;* imagination had done its work, and my health was permanently shattered; neither Bermuda nor any other land can ever bring it back to me. This is my last trip; I am on my way home to die.

LUCK.

IT was at a banquet in London in honor of one of the two or three conspicuously illustrious English military names of this generation. For reasons which will presently appear, I will withhold his real name and titles, and call him Lieutenant-General Lord Arthur Scoresby, Y.C., K.C.B., etc., etc., etc. What a fascination there is in a renowned name! There sat the man, in actual flesh, whom I had heard of so many thousands of times since that day, thirty years before, when his name shot suddenly to the zenith from a Crimean battle-field, to remain forever celebrated. It was food and drink to me to look, and look, and look at that demigod; scanning, searching, noting: the quietness, the reserve, the noble gravity of his countenance; the simple honesty that ex-

[NOTE.—This is not a fancy sketch. I got it from a clergyman who was an instructor at Woolwich forty years ago, and who vouched for its truth.—M. T.]

66

pressed itself all over him; the sweet unconsciousness of his greatness—unconsciousness of
the hundreds of admiring eyes fastened upon
him, unconsciousness of the deep, loving,
sincere worship welling out of the breasts of
those people and flowing toward him.

The clergyman at my left was an old acquaintance of mine—clergyman now, but had
spent the first half of his life in the camp and
field, and as an instructor in the military
school at Woolwich. Just at the moment I
have been talking about, a veiled and singular
light glimmered in his eyes, and he leaned
down and muttered confidentially to me—indicating the hero of the banquet with a gesture,—

"Privately—he's an absolute fool."

This verdict was a great surprise to me. If
its subject had been Napoleon, or Socrates, or
Solomon, my astonishment could not have
been greater. Two things I was well aware
of: that the Reverend was a man of strict
veracity, and that his judgment of men was
good. Therefore I knew, beyond doubt or

question, that the world was mistaken about
this hero: he *was* a fool. So I meant to find
out, at a convenient moment, how the Reverend, all solitary and alone, had discovered
the secret.

Some days later the opportunity came, and
this is what the Reverend told me:

About forty years ago I was an instructor in
the military academy at Woolwich. I was
present in one of the sections when young
Scoresby underwent his preliminary examination. I was touched to the quick with pity;
for the rest of the class answered up brightly
and handsomely, while he—why, dear me, he
didn't know *anything*, so to speak. He was
evidently good, and sweet, and lovable, and
guileless; and so it was exceedingly painful to
see him stand there, as serene as a graven
image, and deliver himself of answers which
were veritably miraculous for stupidity and
ignorance. All the compassion in me was
aroused in his behalf. I said to myself, when
he comes to be examined again, he will be

flung over, of course; so it will be simply a harmless act of charity to ease his fall as much as I can. I took him aside, and found that he knew a little of Cæsar's history; and as he didn't know anything else, I went to work and drilled him like a galley-slave on a certain line of stock questions concerning Cæsar which I knew would be used. If you'll believe me, he went through with flying colors on examination day! He went through on that purely superficial " cram," and got compliments too, while others, who knew a thousand times more than he, got plucked. By some strangely lucky accident—an accident not likely to happen twice in a century—he was asked no question outside of the narrow limits of his drill.

It was stupefying. Well, all through his course I stood by him, with something of the sentiment which a mother feels for a crippled child; and he always saved himself—just by miracle, apparently.

Now of course the thing that would expose him and kill him at last was mathematics. I resolved to make his death as easy as I could;

so I drilled him and crammed him, and crammed him and drilled him, just on the line of
questions which the examiners would be most
likely to use, and then launched him on his
fate. Well, sir, try to conceive of the result:
to my consternation, he took the first prize!
And with it he got a perfect ovation in the
way of compliments.

Sleep? There was no more sleep for me for
a week. My conscience tortured me day and
night. What I had done I had done purely
through charity, and only to ease the poor
youth's fall—I never had dreamed of any such
preposterous result as the thing that had happened. I felt as guilty and miserable as the
creator of Frankenstein. Here was a wooden-
head whom I had put in the way of glittering
promotions and prodigious responsibilities, and
but one thing could happen: he and his responsibilities would all go to ruin together at
the first opportunity.

The Crimean war had just broken out. Of
course there had to be a war, I said to myself:
we couldn't have peace and give this donkey a

chance to die before he is found out. I waited
for the earthquake. It came. And it made
me reel when it did come. He was actually
gazetted to a captaincy in a marching regiment! Better men grow old and gray in the
service before they climb to a sublimity like
that. And who could ever have foreseen that
they would go and put such a load of responsibility on such green and inadequate shoulders? I could just barely have stood it if
they had made him a cornet; but a captain
—think of it! I thought my hair would turn
white.

Consider what I did—I who so loved repose
and inaction. I said to myself, I am responsible to the country for this, and I must go
along with him and protect the country against
him as far as I can. So I took my poor little
capital that I had saved up through years of
work and grinding economy, and went with a
sigh and bought a cornetcy in his regiment,
and away we went to the field.

And there—oh dear, it was awful. Blunders?—why, he never did anything *but* blun-

der. But, you see, nobody was in the fellow's secret—everybody had him focussed wrong, and necessarily misinterpreted his performance every time—consequently they took his idiotic blunders for inspirations of genius; they did, honestly ! His mildest blunders were enough to make a man in his right mind cry; and they did make me cry—and rage and rave too, privately. And the thing that kept me always in a sweat of apprehension was the fact that every fresh blunder he made increased the lustre of his reputation ! I kept saying to my-self, he'll get so high, that when discovery does finally come, it will be like the sun falling out of the sky.

He went right along up, from grade to grade, over the dead bodies of his superiors, until at last, in the hottest moment of the battle of * * * * down went our colonel, and my heart jumped into my mouth, for Scoresby was next in rank ! Now for it, said I; we'll all land in Sheol in ten minutes, sure.

The battle was awfully hot; the allies were steadily giving way all over the field. Our regiment occupied a position that was vital; a blunder now must be destruction. At this crucial moment, what does this immortal fool do but detach the regiment from its place and order a charge over a neighboring hill where there wasn't a suggestion of an enemy ! "There you go !" I said to myself; "this *is* the end at last."

And away we did go, and were over the shoulder of the hill before the insane movement could be discovered and stopped. And what did we find ? An entire and unsuspected Russian army in reserve ! And what happened ? We were eaten up ? That is necessarily what would have happened in ninety-nine cases out of a hundred. But no; those Russians argued that no single regiment would come browsing around there at such a time. It must be the entire English army, and that the sly Russian game was detected and blocked; so they turned tail, and away they went, pell-mell, over the hill and down into the field, in wild confusion, and we after them; they themselves broke the solid Russian centre in the field, and tore through, and in no time there was the most tremendous rout you ever saw, and the defeat of the allies was turned into a sweeping and splendid victory! Marshal Canrobert looked on, dizzy with astonishment, admiration, and delight; and sent right off for Scoresby, and hugged him, and decorated him on the field, in presence of all the armies!

And what was Scoresby's blunder that time? Merely the mistaking his right hand for his left—that was all. An order had come to him to fall back and support our right; and instead, he fell *forward* and went over the hill to the left. But the name he won that day as a marvellous military genius filled the world with his glory, and that glory will never fade while history books last.

He is just as good and sweet and lovable and unpretending as a man can be, but he doesn't know enough to come in when it rains. Now that is absolutely true. He is the supremest ass in the universe; and until half an hour ago nobody knew it but himself and me. He has been pursued, day by day and year by year, by a most phenomenal and astonishing luckiness. He has been a shining soldier in all our wars for a generation; he has littered his whole military life with blunders, and yet has never committed one that didn't make him a knight or a baronet or a lord or something. Look at his breast; why, he is just clothed in domestic and foreign decorations. Well, sir, every one of them is the record of some shouting stupidity or other; and taken together, they are proof that the very best thing in all this world that can befall a man is to be born lucky. I say again, as I said at the banquet, Scoresby's an absolute fool.

THE CAPTAIN'S STORY.

THERE was a good deal of pleasant gossip about old Captain "Hurricane" Jones, of the Pacific Ocean,—peace to his ashes! Two or three of us present had known him; I, particularly well, for I had made four sea-voyages with him. He was a very remarkable man. He was born on a ship; he picked up what little education he had among his shipmates; he began life in the forecastle, and climbed grade by grade to the captaincy. More than fifty years of his sixty-five were spent at sea. He had sailed all oceans, seen all lands, and borrowed a tint from all climates. When a man has been fifty years at sea, he necessarily knows nothing of men, nothing of the world but its surface, nothing of the world's thought, nothing of the world's learning but its A B C, and that blurred and distorted by the unfocussed lenses of an untrained mind. Such a man is only a gray and bearded child. That is what old Hurricane Jones was,—simply an innocent, lovable old infant. When his spirit was in repose he was as sweet and gentle as a girl; when his wrath was up he was a hurricane that made his nickname seem tamely descriptive. He was formidable in a fight, for he was of powerful build and dauntless courage. He was frescoed from head to heel with pictures and mottoes tattooed in red and blue India ink. I was with him one voyage when he got his last vacant space tattooed; this vacant space was around his left ankle. During three days he stumped about the ship with his ankle bare and swollen, and this legend gleaming red and angry out from a clouding of India ink : " Virtue is its own R'd." (There was a lack of room.) He was deeply and sincerely pious, and swore like a fish-woman. He considered swearing blameless, because sailors would not understand an order unillumined by it. He was a profound Biblical scholar,—that is, he thought he was. He believed everything in the Bible, but he had his own methods of arriving at his beliefs. He was of the "advanced" school of thinkers, and applied natural laws to the interpretation of all miracles, somewhat on the plan of the people who make the six days of creation six geological epochs, and so forth. Without being aware of it, he was a rather severe satire on modern scientific religionists. Such a man as I have been describing is rabidly fond of disquisition and argument; one knows that without being told it.

One trip the captain had a clergyman on board, but did not know he was a clergyman, since the passenger list did not betray the fact. He took a great liking to this Rev. Mr. Peters, and talked with him a great deal: told him yarns, gave him toothsome scraps of personal history, and wove a glittering streak of profanity through his garrulous fabric that was refreshing to a spirit weary of the dull neutralities of undecorated speech. One day the captain said, "Peters, do you ever read the Bible?"

"Well—yes."

"I judge it ain't often, by the way you say

it. Now, you tackle it in dead earnest once, and you'll find it'll pay. Don't you get discouraged, but hang right on. First, you won't understand it; but by and by things will begin to clear up, and then you wouldn't lay it down to eat."

" Yes, I have heard that said."

" And it's so, too. There ain't a book that begins with it. It lays over 'em all, Peters. There's some pretty tough things in it,—there ain't any getting around that,—but you stick to them and think them out, and when once you get on the inside everything's plain as day."

" The miracles, too, captain ? "

" Yes, sir ! the miracles, too. Every one of them. Now, there's that business with the prophets of Baal; like enough that stumped you?"

" Well, I don't know but—"

"Own up, now; it stumped you. Well, I don't wonder. You hadn't had any experience in ravelling such things out, and naturally it was too many for you. Would you like to have me explain that thing to you, and show you how to get at the meat of these matters?"

"Indeed, I would, captain, if you don't mind."

Then the captain proceeded as follows : "I'll do it with pleasure. First, you see, I read and read, and thought and thought, till I got to understand what sort of people they were in the old Bible times, and then after that it was clear and easy. Now, this was the way I put it up, concerning Isaac * and the prophets of Baal. There was some mighty sharp men amongst the public characters of that old ancient day, and Isaac was one of them. Isaac had his failings,—plenty of them, too; it ain't for me to apologize for Isaac; he played on the prophets of Baal, and like enough he was justifiable, considering the odds that was against him. No, all I say is, 't wa' n't any miracle, and that I'll show you so's 't you can see it yourself.

" Well, times had been getting rougher and rougher for prophets, — that is, prophets of Isaac's denomination. There were four hun-

* This is the captain's own mistake.

dred and fifty prophets of Baal in the commu-
nity, and only one Presbyterian ; that is, if
Isaac *was* a Presbyterian, which I reckon he
was, but it don't say. Naturally, the prophets
of Baal took all the trade. Isaac was pretty
low-spirited, I reckon, but he was a good deal
of a man, and no doubt he went a-prophesying
around, letting on to be doing a land-office
business, but 't wa' n't any use; he couldn't run
any opposition to amount to anything. By
and by things got desperate with him; he sets
his head to work and thinks it all out, and then
what does he do ? Why, he begins to throw
out hints that the other parties are this and
that and t'other,—nothing very definite, may
be, but just kind of undermining their repûta-
tion in a quiet way. This made talk, of course,
and finally got to the king. The king asked
Isaac what he meant by his talk. Says Isaac,
' Oh, nothing particular; only, can they pray
down fire from heaven on an altar ? It ain't
much, maybe, your majesty, only can they *do*
it ? That's the idea.' So the king was a good
deal disturbed, and he went to the prophets of

Baal, and they said, pretty airy, that if he had
an altar ready, *they* were ready; and they in-
timated he better get it insured, too.

" So next morning all the children of Israel
and their parents and the other people gathered themselves together. Well, here was that
great crowd of prophets of Baal packed together on one side, and Isaac walking up and
down all alone on the other, putting up his
job. When time was called, Isaac let on to be
comfortable and indifferent ; told the other
team to take the first innings. So they went
at it, the whole four hundred and fifty, praying
around the altar, very hopeful, and doing their
level best. They prayed an hour,—two hours,
—three hours,—and so on, plumb till noon. It
wa'n't any use; they had n't took a trick. Of
course they felt kind of ashamed before all
those people, and well they might. Now,
what would a magnanimous man do? Keep
still, wouldn't he? Of course. What did
Isaac do ? He gravelled the prophets of
Baal every way he could think of. Says he,
' You don't speak up loud enough; your god's

asleep, like enough, or may be he's taking a walk; you want to holler, you know,' —or words to that effect; I don't recollect the exact language. Mind, I don't apologize for Isaac; he had his faults.

"Well, the prophets of Baal prayed along the best they knew how all the afternoon, and never raised a spark. At last, about sundown, they were all tuckered out, and they owned up and quit.

"What does Isaac do, now? He steps up and says to some friends of his, there, 'Pour four barrels of water on the altar!' Everybody was astonished; for the other side had prayed at it dry, you know, and got white-washed. They poured it on. Says he, 'Heave on four more barrels.' Then he says, 'Heave on four more.' Twelve barrels, you see, altogether. The water ran all over the altar, and all down the sides, and filled up a trench around it that would hold a couple of hogs-heads,—'measures,' it says; I reckon it means about a hogshead. Some of the people were going to put on their things and go, for they

allowed he was crazy. They didn't know
Isaac. Isaac knelt down and began to pray:
he strung along, and strung along, about the
heathen in distant lands, and about the sister
churches, and about the state and the country
at large, and about those that's in authority in
the government, and all the usual programme,
you know, till everybody had got tired and
gone to thinking about something else, and
then, all of a sudden, when nobody was noticing, he outs with a match and rakes it on the
under side of his leg, and pff! up the whole
thing blazes like a house afire! Twelve barrels of *water?* *Petroleum*, sir, PETROLEUM!
that's what it was!"

"Petroleum, captain?"

"Yes, sir; the country was full of it. Isaac
knew all about that. You read the Bible.
Don't you worry about the tough places.
They ain't tough when you come to think
them out and throw light on them. There
ain't a thing in the Bible but what is true; all
you want is to go prayerfully to work and
cipher out how 't was done."

A CURIOUS EXPERIENCE.

THIS is the story which the Major told me, as nearly as I can recall it:—

In the winter of 1862–3, I was commandant of Fort Trumbull, at New London, Conn. Maybe our life there was not so brisk as life at "the front"; still it was brisk enough, in its way—one's brains did n't cake together there for lack of something to keep them stirring. For one thing, all the Northern atmosphere at that time was thick with mysterious rumors— rumors to the effect that rebel spies were flitting everywhere, and getting ready to blow up our Northern forts, burn our hotels, send infected clothing into our towns, and all that sort of thing. You remember it. All this had a tendency to keep us awake, and knock the traditional dulness out of garrison life. Besides, ours was a recruiting station—which is the same as saying we had n't any time to waste in dozing, or dreaming, or fooling around. Why, with all our watchfulness, fifty per cent. of a day's recruits would leak out of our hands and give us the slip the same night. The bounties were so prodigious that a recruit could pay a sentinel three or four hundred dollars to let him escape, and still have enough of his bounty-money left to constitute a fortune for a poor man. Yes, as I said before, our life was not drowsy.

Well, one day I was in my quarters alone, doing some writing, when a pale and ragged lad of fourteen or fifteen entered, made a neat bow, and said,—

" I believe recruits are received here ? "

" Yes."

" Will you please enlist me, sir ? "

" Dear me, no ! You are too young, my boy, and too small."

A disappointed look came into his face, and quickly deepened into an expression of despondency. He turned slowly away, as if to go; hesitated, then faced me again, and said, in a tone which went to my heart,—

"I have no home, and not a friend in the world. If you *could* only enlist me!"

But of course the thing was out of the question, and I said so as gently as I could. Then I told him to sit down by the stove and warm himself, and added,—

"You shall have something to eat, presently. You are hungry?"

He did not answer; he did not need to; the gratitude in his big soft eyes was more eloquent than any words could have been. He sat down by the stove, and I went on writing. Occasionally I took a furtive glance at him. I noticed that his clothes and shoes, although soiled and damaged, were of good style and material. This fact was suggestive. To it I added the facts that his voice was low and musical; his eyes deep and melancholy; his carriage and address gentlemanly; evidently the poor chap was in trouble. As a result, I was interested.

However, I became absorbed in my work, by and by, and forgot all about the boy. I don't know how long this lasted; but, at length,

I happened to look up. The boy's back was toward me, but his face was turned in such a way that I could see one of his cheeks—and down that cheek a rill of noiseless tears was flowing.

"God bless my soul!" I said to myself; "I forgot the poor rat was starving." Then I made amends for my brutality by saying to him, "Come along, my lad; you shall dine with *me;* I am alone to-day."

He gave me another of those grateful looks, and a happy light broke in his face. At the table he stood with his hand on his chair-back until I was seated, then seated himself. I took up my knife and fork and—well, I simply held them, and kept still; for the boy had inclined his head and was saying a silent grace. A thousand hallowed memories of home and my childhood poured in upon me, and I sighed to think how far I had drifted from religion and its balm for hurt minds, its comfort and solace and support.

As our meal progressed, I observed that young Wicklow—Robert Wicklow was his full

name—knew what to do with his napkin; and
—well, in a word, I observed that he was a
boy of good breeding; never mind the details.
He had a simple frankness, too, which won
upon me. We talked mainly about himself,
and I had no difficulty in getting his history
out of him. When he spoke of his having
been born and reared in Louisiana, I warmed
to him decidedly, for I had spent some time
down there. I knew all the " coast " region of
the Mississippi, and loved it, and had not been
long enough away from it for my interest in it
to begin to pale. The very names that fell
from his lips sounded good to me,—so good
that I steered the talk in directions that would
bring them out. Baton Rouge, Plaquemine,
Donaldsonville, Sixty - mile Point, Bonnet-
Carre, the Stock - Landing, Carrollton, the
Steamship Landing, the Steamboat Landing,
New Orleans, Tchoupitoulas Street, the Es-
planade, the Rue des Bons Enfants, the St.
Charles Hotel, the Tivoli Circle, the Shell
Road, Lake Pontchartrain; and it was particularly delightful to me to hear once more of the

"R. E. Lee,' the "Natchez," the "Eclipse," the "General Quitman," the "Duncan F. Kenner," and other old familiar steamboats. It was almost as good as being back there, these names so vividly reproduced in my mind the look of the things they stood for. Briefly, this was little Wicklow's history:—

When the war broke out, he and his invalid aunt and his father were living near Baton Rouge, on a great and rich plantation which had been in the family for fifty years. The father was a Union man. He was persecuted in all sorts of ways, but clung to his principles. At last, one night, masked men burned his mansion down, and the family had to fly for their lives. They were hunted from place to place, and learned all there was to know about poverty, hunger, and distress. The invalid aunt found relief at last: misery and exposure killed her; she died in an open field, like a tramp, the rain beating upon her and the thunder booming overhead. Not long afterward, the father was captured by an armed band; and while the son begged and pleaded, the victim was strung up before his face. [At this point a baleful light shone in the youth's eyes, and he said, with the manner of one who talks to himself: " If I cannot be enlisted, no matter —I shall find a way—I shall find a way."] As soon as the father was pronounced dead, the son was told that if he was not out of that region within twenty-four hours, it would go hard with him. That night he crept to the riverside and hid himself near a plantation landing. By and by the " Duncan F. Kenner," stopped there, and he swam out and concealed himself in the yawl that was dragging at her stern. Before daylight the boat reached the Stock-Landing, and he slipped ashore. He walked the three miles which lay between that point and the house of an uncle of his in Good-Children Street, in New Orleans, and then his troubles were over for the time being. But this uncle was a Union man, too, and before very long he concluded that he had better leave the South. So he and young Wicklow slipped out of the country on board a sailing vessel, and in due time reached New York.

They put up at the Astor House. Young
Wicklow had a good time of it for a while,
strolling up and down Broadway, and observ-
ing the strange Northern sights; but in the
end a change came,—and not for the better.
The uncle had been cheerful at first, but now he
began to look troubled and despondent; moreover, he became moody and irritable; talked
of money giving out, and no way to get more,
—"not enough left for one, let alone two."
Then, one morning, he was missing—did not
come to breakfast. The boy inquired at the
office, and was told that the uncle had paid his
bill the night before and gone away—to Boston, the clerk believed, but was not certain.

The lad was alone and friendless. He did
not know what to do, but concluded he had
better try to follow and find his uncle. He
went down to the steamboat landing; learned
that the trifle of money in his pocket would not
carry him to Boston; however, it would carry
him to New London; so he took passage for
that port, resolving to trust to Providence to
furnish him means to travel the rest of the way.

He had now been wandering about the streets of New London three days and nights, getting a bite and a nap here and there for charity's sake. But he had given up at last; courage and hope were both gone. If he could enlist, nobody could be more thankful; if he could not get in as a soldier, couldn't he be a drummer-boy? Ah, he would work *so* hard to please, and would be so grateful !

Well, there's the history of young Wicklow, just as he told it to me, barring details. I said,—

"My boy, you are among friends, now,— don't you be troubled any more." How his eyes glistened ! I called in Sergeant John Rayburn,—he was from Hartford; lives in Hartford yet; maybe you know him,—and said, "Rayburn, quarter this boy with the musicians. I am going to enroll him as a drummer-boy, and I want you to look after him and see that he is well treated."

Well, of course, intercourse between the commandant of the post and the drummer-boy came to an end, now; but the poor little

friendless chap lay heavy on my heart, just the
same. I kept on the lookout, hoping to see
him brighten up and begin to be cheery and
gay; but no, the days went by, and there was
no change. He associated with nobody; he
was always absent-minded, always thinking;
his face was always sad. One morning Rayburn asked leave to speak to me privately.
Said he,—

"I hope I don't offend, sir; but the truth is,
the musicians are in such a sweat it seems as if
somebody's *got* to speak."

"Why, what is the trouble?"

"It's the Wicklow boy, sir. The musicians
are down on him to an extent you can't imagine."

"Well, go on, go on. What has he been
doing?"

"Prayin', sir."

"Praying!"

"Yes, sir; the musicians haven't any peace
of their life for that boy's prayin'. First thing
in the morning he's at it; noons he's at it; and
nights—well, *nights* he just lays into 'em like

all possessed ! Sleep ? Bless you, they *can't* sleep: he's got the floor, as the sayin' is, and then when he once gets his supplication-mill agoin', there just simply ain't any let-up *to* him. He starts in with the band-master, and he prays for him; next he takes the head bugler, and he prays for him; next the bass drum, and he scoops *him* in; and so on, right straight through the band, givin' them all a show, and takin' that amount of interest in it which would make you think he thought he warn't but a little while for this world, and believed he couldn't be happy in heaven without he had a brass band along, and wanted to pick 'em out for himself, so he could depend on 'em to do up the national tunes in a style suitin' to the place. Well, sir, heavin' boots at him don't have no effect; it's dark in there; and, besides, he don't pray fair, anyway, but kneels down behind the big drum; so it don't make no difference if they *rain* boots at him, *he* don't give a dern—warbles right along, same as if it was applause. They sing out, 'Oh, dry up !' 'Give us a rest !' 'Shoot him !' 'Oh, take a walk !'

and all sorts of such things.   But what of it?
It don't phaze him. *He* don't mind it."   After
a pause : " Kind of a good little fool, too ; gits
up in the mornin' and carts all that stock of
boots back, and sorts 'em out and sets each
man's pair where they belong.   And they've
been throwed at him so much now, that he
knows every boot in the band,—can sort 'em
out with his eyes shut."

After another pause, which I forebore to
interrupt,—

"But the roughest thing about it is, that
when he's done prayin',—when he ever *does*
get done,—he pipes up and begins to *sing*.
Well, you know what a honey kind of a voice
he's got when he talks; you know how it
would persuade a cast-iron dog to come down
off of a doorstep and lick his hand.   Now if
you'll take my word for it, sir, it ain't a circumstance to his singin'!   Flute music is harsh to
that boy's singin'.   Oh, he just gurgles it out
so soft and sweet and low, there in the dark,
that it makes you think you are in heaven."

"What is there ' rough ' about that?"

" Ah, that's just it, sir. You hear him sing

" ' Just as I am—poor, wretched, blind,'

—just you hear him sing that, once, and see if
you don't melt all up and the water come into
your eyes ! I don't care *what* he sings, it goes
plum straight home to you—it goes deep down
to where you *live*—and it fetches you every
time ! Just you hear him sing :—

> " ' Child of sin and sorrow, filled with dismay,
>   Wait not till to-morrow, yield thee to-day;
>   Grieve not that love
>   Which, from above '—

and so on. It makes a body feel like the
wickedest, ungratefulest brute that walks.
And when he sings them songs of his about
home, and mother, and childhood, and old
memories, and things that's vanished, and old
friends dead and gone, it fetches everything
before your face that you've ever loved and
lost in all your life—and it's just beautiful, it's
just divine to listen to, sir—but, Lord, Lord,
the heart-break of it ! The band—well, they
all cry—every rascal of them blubbers, and

don't try to hide it, either; and first you know,
that very gang that's been slammin' boots at
that boy will skip out of their bunks all of a
sudden, and rush over in the dark and hug
him! Yes, they do—and slobber all over him,
and call him pet names, and beg him to for-
give them. And just at that time, if a regiment was to offer to hurt a hair of that cub's
head, they'd go for that regiment, if it was a
whole army corps!"

Another pause.

"Is that all?" said I.

"Yes, sir."

"Well, dear me, what is the complaint?
What do they want done?"

"Done? Why, bless you, sir, they want
you to stop him from *singin'*."

"What an idea! You said his music was
divine."

"That's just it. It's *too* divine. Mortal man
can't stand it. It stirs a body up so; it turns a
body inside out; it racks his feelin's all to
rags; it makes him feel bad and wicked, and
not fit for any place but perdition. It keeps a

body in such an everlastin' state of repentin', that nothin' don't taste good and there ain't no comfort in life. And then the *cryin'*, you see —every mornin' they are ashamed to look one another in the face."

"Well, this is an odd case, and a singular complaint. So they really want the singing stopped?"

"Yes, sir, that is the idea. They don't wish to ask too much; they would like powerful well to have the prayin' shut down on, or leastways trimmed off around the edges; but the main thing's the singin'. If they can only get the singin' choked off, they think they can stand the prayin', rough as it is to be bully-ragged so much that way."

I told the sergeant I would take the matter under consideration. That night I crept into the musicians' quarters and listened. The sergeant had not overstated the case. I heard the praying voice pleading in the dark; I heard the execrations of the harassed men; I heard the rain of boots whiz through the air, and bang and thump around the big drum.

The thing touched me, but it amused me, too. By and by, after an impressive silence, came the singing. Lord, the pathos of it, the enchantment of it! Nothing in the world was ever so sweet, so gracious, so tender, so holy, so moving. I made my stay very brief; I was beginning to experience emotions of a sort not proper to the commandant of a fortress.

Next day I issued orders which stopped the praying and singing. Then followed three or four days which were so full of bounty-jumping excitements and irritations that I never once thought of my drummer-boy. But now comes Sergeant Rayburn, one morning, and says,—

" That new boy acts mighty strange, sir."

" How ? "

" Well, sir, he's all the time writing."

" Writing ? What does he write—letters ? "

" I don't know, sir; but whenever he's off duty, he is always poking and nosing around the fort, all by himself,—blest if I think there's a hole or corner in it he hasn't been into,—and every little while he outs with pencil and paper and scribbles something down."

This gave me a most unpleasant sensation. I wanted to scoff at it, but it was not a time to scoff at *anything* that had the least suspicious tinge about it. Things were happening all around us, in the North, then, that warned us to be always on the alert, and always suspecting. I recalled to mind the suggestive fact that this boy was from the South,—the extreme South, Louisiana,—and the thought was not of a re-assuring nature, under the circumstances. Nevertheless, it cost me a pang to give the orders which I now gave to Rayburn. I felt like a father who plots to expose his own child to shame and injury. I told Rayburn to keep quiet, bide his time, and get me some of those writings whenever he could manage it without the boy's finding it out. And I charged him not to do anything which might let the boy discover that he was being watched. I also ordered that he allow the lad his usual liber-ties, but that he be followed at a distance when he went out into the town.

During the next two days, Rayburn report-ed to me several times. No success. The

boy was still writing, but he always pocketed
his paper with a careless air whenever Rayburn appeared in his vicinity. He had gone
twice to an old deserted stable in the town,
remained a minute or two, and come out
again. One could not pooh-pooh these things
—they had an evil look. I was obliged to
confess to myself that I was getting uneasy.
I went into my private quarters and sent for
my second in command—an officer of intelli-
gence and judgment, son of General James
Watson Webb. He was surprised and troubled. We had a long talk over the matter, and
came to the conclusion that it would be worth
while to institute a secret search. I determined to take charge of that myself. So I
had myself called at two in the morning; and,
pretty soon after, I was in the musicians' quarters, crawling along the floor on my stomach
among the snorers. I reached my slumbering
waif's bunk at last, without disturbing anybody, captured his clothes and kit, and crawled
stealthily back again. When I got to my own
quarters, I found Webb there, waiting and

eager to know the result. We made search immediately. The clothes were a disappoint-ment. In the pockets we found blank paper and a pencil; nothing else, except a jack-knife and such queer odds and ends and use-less trifles as boys hoard and value. We turned to the kit hopefully. Nothing there but a rebuke for us!—a little Bible with this written on the fly-leaf: "Stranger, be kind to my boy, for his mother's sake."

I looked at Webb—he dropped his eyes; he looked at me—I dropped mine. Neither spoke. I put the book reverently back in its place. Presently Webb got up and went away, with-out remark. After a little I nerved myself up to my unpalatable job, and took the plunder back to where it belonged, crawling on my stomach as before. It seemed the peculiarly appropriate attitude for the business I was in.

I was most honestly glad when it was over and done with.

About noon next day Rayburn came, as usu-al, to report. I cut him short. I said,—

" Let this nonsense be dropped.   We are making a bugaboo oút of a poor little cub who has got no more harm in him than a hymn-book."

The sergeant looked surprised, and said,—

" Well, you know it was your orders, sir, and I've got some of the writing."

"And what does it amount to ?   How did you get it ? "

" I peeped through the key-hole, and see him writing.   So when I judged he was about done, I made a sort of a little cough, and I see him crumple it up and throw it in the fire, and look all around to see if anybody was com-ing.   Then he settled back as comfortable and careless as anything.   Then I comes in, and passes the time of day pleasantly, and sends him of an errand.   He never looked uneasy, but went right along.   It was a coal-fire and new-built; the writing had gone over behind a chunk, out of sight; but I got it out; there it is; it ain't hardly scorched, you see."

I glanced at the paper and took in a sentence or two.   Then I dismissed the sergeant and told him to send Webb to me. Here is the paper in full :—

" FORT TRUMBULL, the 8th.

" COLONEL,—I was mistaken as to the calibre of the three guns I ended my list with.   They are 18-pounders; all the rest of the armament is as I stated.   The garrison remains as before reported, except that the two light infantry companies that were to be detached for service at the front are to stay here for the present —can't find out for how long, just now, but will soon. We are satisfied that. all things considered, matters had better be postponed un—"

There it broke off—there is where Rayburn coughed and interrupted the writer. / All my affection for the boy, all my respect for him and charity for his forlorn condition, withered in a moment under the blight of this revelation of cold-blooded baseness.

But never mind about that. Here was business,—business that required profound and immediate attention, too.   Webb and I turned the subject over and over, and examined it all around. Webb said,—

" What a pity he was interrupted ! Something is going to be postponed until—when ? And what *is* the something ? Possibly he

would have mentioned it, the pious little rep-
tile!"

"Yes," I said, "we have missed a trick.
And who is '*we*,' in the letter? Is it conspirators inside the fort or outside?"

That "we" was uncomfortably suggestive.
However, it was not worth while to be guess-
ing around that, so we proceeded to matters
more practical. In the first place, we decided
to double the sentries and keep the strictest
possible watch. Next, we thought of calling
Wicklow in and making him divulge everything; but that did not seem wisest until other
methods should fail. We must have some more
of the writings; so we began to plan to that
end. And now we had an idea: Wicklow
never went to the post-office,—perhaps the deserted stable was his post-office. We sent for
my confidential clerk—a young German named
Sterne, who was a sort of natural detective—
and told him all about the case and ordered
him to go to work on it. Within the hour we
got word that Wicklow was writing again.
Shortly afterward, word came that he had

asked leave to go out into the town. He was detained awhile, and meantime Sterne hurried off and concealed himself in the stable. By and by he saw Wicklow saunter in, look about him, then hide something under some rubbish in a corner, and take leisurely leave again. Sterne pounced upon the hidden article—a letter—and brought it to us. It had no superscription and no signature. It repeated what we had already read, and then went on to say :—

" We think it best to postpone till the two companies are gone. I mean the four inside think so; have not communicated with the others—afraid of attracting attention. I say four because we have lost two; they had hardly enlisted and got inside when they were shipped off to the front. It will be absolutely necessary to have two in their places. The two that went were the brothers from Thirty-mile Point. I have something of the greatest importance to reveal, but must not trust it to this method of communication; will try the other."

" The little scoundrel ! " said Webb; "who *could* have supposed he was a spy ? However, never mind about that; let us add up our particulars, such as they are, and see how the case stands to date. First, we've got a rebel spy in

our midst, whom we know; secondly, we've
got three more in our midst whom we don't
know; thirdly, these spies have been introduced among us through the simple and easy
process of enlisting as soldiers in the Union
army—and evidently two of them have got
sold at it, and been shipped off to the front;
fourthly, there are assistant spies ' outside '—
number indefinite; fifthly, Wicklow has very
important matter which he is afraid to communicate by the ' present method '—will ' try the
other.'   That is the case, as it now stands.
Shall we collar Wicklow and make him confess ?   Or shall we catch the person who re-
moves the letters from the stable and make *him*
tell ?   Or shall we keep still and find out
more ? "

We decided upon the last course. We
judged that we did not need to proceed to
summary measures now, since it was evident
that the conspirators were likely to wait till
those two light infantry companies were out of
the way.   We fortified Sterne with pretty
ample powers, and told him to use his best en-

deavors to find out Wicklow's "other method" of communication. We meant to play a bold game; and to this end we proposed to keep the spies in an unsuspecting state as long as possible. So we ordered Sterne to return to the stable immediately, and, if he found the coast clear, to conceal Wicklow's letter where it was before, and leave it there for the conspirators to get.

The night closed down without further event. It was cold and dark and sleety, with a raw wind blowing; still I turned out of my warm bed several times during the night, and went the rounds in person, to see that all was right and that every sentry was on the alert. I always found them wide awake and watchful; evidently whispers of mysterious dangers had been floating about, and the doubling of the guards had been a kind of indorsement of those rumors. Once, toward morning, I encountered Webb, breasting his way against the bitter wind, and learned then that he, also, had been the rounds several times to see that all was going right.

Next day's events hurried things up somewhat. Wicklow wrote another letter; Sterne
preceded him to the stable and saw him deposit it; captured it as soon as Wicklow was
out of the way, then slipped out and followed
the little spy at a distance, with a detective in
plain clothes at his own heels, for we thought
it judicious to have the law's assistance handy
in case of need. Wicklow went to the railway
station, and waited around till the train from
New York came in, then stood scanning the
faces of the crowd as they poured out of the
cars. Presently an aged gentleman, with green
goggles and a cane, came limping along, stopped in Wicklow's neighborhood, and began to
look about him expectantly. In an instant
Wicklow darted forward, thrust an envelope
into his hand, then glided away and disap-
peared in the throng. The next instant
Sterne had snatched the letter; and as he hurried past the detective, he said: " Follow the
old gentleman—don't lose sight of him." Then
Sterne skurried out with the crowd, and came
straight to the fort.

We sat with closed doors, and instructed the guard outside to allow no interruption.

First we opened the letter captured at the stable.   It read as follows:—

" HOLY ALLIANCE,—Found, in the usual gun, commands from the Master, left there last night, which set aside the instructions heretofore received from the subordinate quarter.   Have left in the gun the usual indication that the commands reached the proper hand—"

Webb, interrupting: " Is n't the boy under constant surveillance now ?"

I said yes; he had been under strict surveillance ever since the capturing of his former letter.

" Then how could he put anything into a gun, or take anything out of it, and not get caught ?"

" Well," I said, " I don't like the look of that very well."

" I don't, either," said Webb.   " It simply means that there are conspirators among the very sentinels.   Without their connivance in some way or other, the thing could n't have been done."

I sent for Rayburn, and ordered him to examine the batteries and see what he could find. The reading of the letter was then resumed:—

"The new commands are peremptory, and require that the MMMM shall be FFFFF at 3 o'clock to-morrow morning. Two hundred will arrive, in small parties, by train and otherwise, from various directions, and will be at appointed place at right time. I will distribute the sign to-day. Success is apparently sure, though something must have got out, for the sentries have been doubled, and the chiefs went the rounds last night several times. W. W. comes from southerly to-day and will receive secret orders—by the other method. All six of you must be in 166 at sharp 2 A. M. You will find B. B. there, who will give you detailed instructions. Password same as last time, only reversed—put first syllable last and last syllable first. REMEMBER XXXX. Do not forget. Be of good heart; before the next sun rises you will be heroes; your fame will be permanent; you will have added a deathless page to history. Amen."

" Thunder and Mars," said Webb, " but we are getting into mighty hot quarters, as I look at it ! "

I said there was no question but that things were beginning to wear a most serious aspect. Said I,—

" A desperate enterprise is on foot, that is plain enough. To-night is the time set for it, —that, also, is plain. The exact nature of the enterprise—I mean the manner of it—is hidden away under those blind bunches of M's and F's, but the end and aim, I judge, is the surprise and capture of the post. We must move quick and sharp now. I think nothing can be gained by continuing our clandestine policy as regards Wicklow. We *must* know, and as soon as possible, too, where ' 166 ' is located, so that we can make a descent upon the gang there at 2 A. M.; and doubtless the quickest way to get that information will be to force it out of that boy. But first of all, and before we make any important move, I must lay the facts before the War Department, and ask for plenary powers."

The despatch was prepared in cipher to go over the wires; I read it, approved it, and sent it along.

We presently finished discussing the letter which was under consideration, and then opened the one which had been snatched from the lame gentleman. It contained nothing but a couple of perfectly blank sheets of note-paper! It was a chilly check to our hot eagerness and expectancy. We felt as blank as the paper, for a moment, and twice as foolish. But it was for a moment only; for, of course, we immediately afterward thought of "sympathetic ink." We held the paper close to the fire and watched for the characters to come out, under the influence of the heat; but nothing appeared but some faint tracings, which we could make nothing of. We then called in the surgeon, and sent him off with orders to apply every test he was acquainted with till he got the right one, and report the contents of the letter to me the instant he brought them to the surface. This check was a confounded annoyance, and we naturally chafed under the delay; for we had fully expected to get out of that letter some of the most important secrets of the plot.

Now appeared Sergeant Rayburn, and drew from his pocket a piece of twine string about a foot long, with three knots tied in it, and held it up.

" I got it out of a gun on the water-front,"
said he.   " I took the tompions out of all the
guns and examined close; this string was the
only thing that was in any gun."

So this bit of string was Wicklow's " sign " to
signify that the " Master's " commands had not
miscarried.   I ordered that every sentinel who
had served near that gun during the past twenty-four hours be put in confinement at once and
separately, and not allowed to communicate
with any one without my privity and consent.

A telegram now came from the Secretary of
War.   It read as follows :—

" Suspend *habeas corpus*.   Put town under martial
law.   Make necessary arrests.   Act with vigor and
promptness.   Keep the Department informed."

We were now in shape to go to work.   I
sent out and had the lame gentleman quietly
arrested and as quietly brought into the fort;
I placed him under guard, and forbade speech
to him or from him.   He was inclined to bluster at first, but he soon dropped that.

Next came word that Wicklow had been
seen to give something to a couple of our new

recruits; and that, as soon as his back was turned, these had been seized and confined. Upon each was found a small bit of paper, bearing these words and signs in pencil :—

EAGLE'S THIRD FLIGHT.

REMEMBER XXXX.

166.

In accordance with instructions, I telegraphed to the Department, in cipher, the progress made, and also described the above ticket. We seemed to be in a strong enough position now to venture to throw off the mask as regarded Wicklow ; so I sent for him. I also sent for and received back the letter written in sympathetic ink, the surgeon accompanying it with the information that thus far it had resisted his tests, but that there were others he could apply when I should be ready for him to do so.

Presently Wicklow entered. He had a

somewhat worn and anxious look, but he was composed and easy, and if he suspected anything it did not appear in his face or manner. I allowed him to stand there a moment or two, then I said pleasantly,—

" My boy, why do you go to that old stable so much ? "

He answered, with simple demeanor and without embarrassment,—

" Well, I hardly know, sir; there isn't any particular reason, except that I like to be alone, and I amuse myself there."

" You amuse yourself there, do you ? "

" Yes, sir," he replied, as innocently and simply as before.

" Is that all you do there ? "

" Yes, sir," he said, looking up with childlike wonderment in his big soft eyes.

" You are *sure ?* "

" Yes, sir, sure."

After a pause, I said,—

" Wicklow, why do you write so much ? "

" I ?   I do not write much, sir."

" You don't ? "

" No, sir.   Oh, if you mean scribbling, I *do* scribble some, for amusement."

" What do you do with your scribblings ? "

" Nothing, sir—throw them away."

" Never send them to anybody ? "

" No, sir."

I suddenly thrust before him the letter to the " Colonel."   He started slightly, but immediately composed himself. A slight tinge spread itself over his cheek.

" How came you to send *this* piece of scribbling, then ? "

" I nev—never meant any harm, sir."

" Never meant any harm !   You betray the armament and condition of the post, and mean no harm by it ? "

He hung his head and was silent.

" Come, speak up, and stop lying. Whom was this letter intended for ? "

He showed signs of distress, now ; but quickly collected himself, and replied, in a tone of deep earnestness,—

" I will tell you the truth, sir—the whole truth. The letter was never intended for anybody at all. I wrote it only to amuse myself. I see the error and foolishness of it, now,—but it is the only offence, sir, upon my honor."

" Ah, I am glad of that. It is dangerous to be writing such letters. I hope you are sure this is the only one you wrote ? "

" Yes, sir, perfectly sure."

His hardihood was stupefying. He told that lie with as sincere a countenance as any creature ever wore. I waited a moment to soothe down my rising temper, and then said,—

" Wicklow, jog your memory now, and see if you can help me with two or three little matters which I wish to inquire about."

" I will do my very best, sir."

" Then, to begin with—who is ' the Master ' ? "

It betrayed him into darting a startled glance at our faces, but that was all. He was serene again in a moment, and tranquilly answered,—

"I do not know, sir."

" You do not know ? "

"I do not know."

" You are *sure* you do not know ? "

He tried hard to keep his eyes on mine, but the strain was too great; his chin sunk slowly toward his breast and he was silent; he stood there nervously fumbling with a button, an object to command one's pity, in spite of his base acts.   Presently I broke the stillness with the question,—

" Who are the ' Holy Alliance' ? "

His body shook visibly, and he made a slight random gesture with his hands, which to me was like the appeal of a despairing creature for compassion.   But he made no sound.   He continued to stand with his face bent toward the ground.   As we sat gazing at him, waiting for him to speak, we saw the big tears begin to roll down his cheeks.   But he remained silent.   After a little, I said,—

" You must answer me, my boy, and you must tell me the truth.   Who are the Holy Alliance ? "

He wept on in silence.   Presently I said, somewhat sharply,—

" Answer the question ! "

He struggled to get command of his voice; and then, looking up appealingly, forced the words out between his sobs,—

"Oh, have pity on me, sir !   I cannot answer it, for I do not know."

"What !"

"Indeed, sir, I am telling the truth.   I never have heard of the Holy Alliance till this moment.   On my honor, sir, this is so."

"Good heavens !   Look at this second letter of yours; there, do you see those words, '*Holy Alliance ?*'   What do you say now ?"

He gazed up into my face with the hurt look of one upon whom a great wrong had been wrought, then said, feelingly,—

"This is some cruel joke, sir; and how could they play it upon me, who have tried all I could to do right, and have never done harm to anybody ?   Some one has counterfeited my hand; I never wrote a line of this; I have never seen this letter before !"

"Oh, you unspeakable liar !   Here, what do you say to *this ?*"—and I snatched the sympathetic-ink letter from my pocket and thrust it before his eyes.

His face turned white !—as white as a dead person's. He wavered slightly in his tracks, and put his hand against the wall to steady himself. After a moment he asked, in so faint a voice that it was hardly audible,—

"Have you—read it ?"

Our faces must have answered the truth before my lips could get out a false "yes," for I distinctly saw the courage come back into that boy's eyes. I waited for him to say something, but he kept silent. So at last I said,—

" Well, what have you to say as to the revelations in this letter ?"

He answered, with perfect composure,—

" Nothing, except that they are entirely harmless and innocent; they can hurt nobody."

I was in something of a corner now, as I couldn't disprove his assertion. I did not know exactly how to proceed. However, an idea came to my relief, and I said,—

" You are sure you know nothing about the

Master and the Holy Alliance, and did not write the letter which you say is a forgery ? "

" Yes, sir—sure."

I slowly drew out the knotted twine string and held it up without speaking. He gazed at it indifferently, then looked at me inquiringly. My patience was sorely taxed. However, I kept my temper down, and said in my usual voice,—

" Wicklow, do you see this ? "

" Yes, sir."

" What is it ? "

" It seems to be a piece of string."

" *Seems ?* It *is* a piece of string. Do you recognize it ? "

" No, sir," he replied, as calmly as the words could be uttered.

His coolness was perfectly wonderful ! I paused now for several seconds, in order that the silence might add impressiveness to what I was about to say ; then I rose and laid my hand on his shoulder, and said gravely,—

" It will do you no good, poor boy, none in the world. This sign to the ' Master,' this knotted string, found in one of the guns on the water-front—"

" Found *in* the gun ! Oh, no, no, no ! do not say *in* the gun, but in a crack in the tompion ! —it *must* have been in the crack ! " and down he went on his knees and clasped his hands and lifted up a face that was pitiful to see, so ashy it was, and wild with terror.

" No, it was *in* the gun."

" Oh, something has gone wrong ! My God, I am lost ! " and he sprang up and darted this way and that, dodging the hands that were put out to catch him, and doing his best to escape from the place. But of course escape was impossible. Then he flung himself on his knees again, crying with all his might, and clasped me around the legs; and so he clung to me and begged and pleaded, saying, " Oh, have pity on me ! Oh, be merciful to me ! Do not betray me; they would not spare my life a moment ! Protect me, save me. I will confess everything ! "

It took us some time to quiet him down and modify his fright, and get him into some-

thing like a rational frame of mind. Then
I began to question him, he answering
humbly, with downcast eyes, and from time
to time swabbing away his constantly flowing tears.

" So you are at heart a rebel ? "

" Yes, sir."

" And a spy ? "

" Yes, sir."

" And have been acting under distinct orders from outside ? "

" Yes, sir."

" Willingly ? "

" Yes, sir."

" *Gladly*, perhaps ? "

" Yes, sir ; it would do no good to deny it.
The South is my country ; my heart is Southern, and it is all in her cause."

" Then the tale you told me of your wrongs
and the persecution of your family was made
up for the occasion ? "

" They—they told me to say it, sir."

" And you would betray and destroy those
who pitied and sheltered you. Do you com-

prehend how base you are, you poor misguided
thing ? "

He replied with sobs only.

" Well, let that pass.   To business.   Who is
the 'Colonel,' and where is he ? "

He began to cry hard, and tried to beg off
from answering.   He said he would be killed
if he told.   I threatened to put him in the dark
cell and lock him up if he did not come out
with the information.   At the same time I
promised to protect him from all harm if he
made a clean breast.   For all answer, he closed
his mouth firmly and put on a stubborn air
which I could not bring him out of.   At last I
started with him; but a single glance into the
dark cell converted him.   He broke into a
passion of weeping and supplicating, and declared he would tell everything.

So I brought him back, and he named the
" Colonel," and described him particularly.
Said he would be found at the principal hotel
in the town, in citizen's dress.   I had to
threaten him again, before he would describe
and name the " Master."   Said the Master

would be found at No. 15 Bond Street, New York, passing under the name of R. F. Gaylord. I telegraphed name and description to the chief of police of the metropolis, and asked that Gaylord be arrested and held till I could send for him.

" Now," said I, " it seems that there are several of the conspirators ' outside,' presumably in New London. Name and describe them."

He named and described three men and two women,—all stopping at the principal hotel. I sent out quietly, and had them and the " Colonel " arrested and confined in the fort.

" Next, I want to know all about your three fellow-conspirators who are here in the fort."

He was about to dodge me with a falsehood, I thought; but I produced the mysterious bits of paper which had been found upon two of them, and this had a salutary effect upon him. I said we had possession of two of the men, and he must point out the third. This frightened him badly, and he cried out,—

" Oh, please don't make me ; he would kill me on the spot ! "

I said that that was all nonsense; I would
have somebody near by to protect him, and,
besides, the men should be assembled without
arms. I ordered all the raw recruits to be
mustered, and then the poor trembling little
wretch went out and stepped along down the
line, trying to look as indifferent as possible.
Finally he spoke a single word to one of the
men, and before he had gone five steps the
man was under arrest.

As soon as Wicklow was with us again, I
had those three men brought in.   I made one
of them stand forward, and said,—

"Now, Wicklow, mind, not a shade's diver-
gence from the exact truth.   Who is this man,
and what do you know about him?"

Being "in for it," he cast consequences aside,
fastened his eyes on the man's face, and spoke
straight along without hesitation,—to the following effect.

"His real name is George Bristow. He is
from New Orleans; was second mate of the
coast-packet 'Capitol,' two years ago ; is a
desperate character, and has served two terms

for manslaughter,—one for killing a deck-hand named Hyde with a capstan-bar, and one for killing a roustabout for refusing to heave the lead, which is no part of a roustabout's business. He is a spy, and was sent here by the Colonel, to act in that capacity. He was third mate of the 'St. Nicholas,' when she blew up in the neighborhood of Memphis, in '58, and came near being lynched for robbing the dead and wounded while they were being taken ashore in an empty wood-boat."

And so forth and so on—he gave the man's biography in full. When he had finished, I said to the man,—

" What have you to say to this ? "

" Barring your presence, sir, it is the infernalcst lie that ever was spoke ! "

I sent him back into confinement, and called the others forward in turn. Same result. The boy gave a detailed history of each, without ever hesitating for a word or a fact; but all I could get out of either rascal was the indignant assertion that it was all a lie. They would confess nothing. I returned them to captivity, and brought out the rest of my prisoners, one by one. Wicklow told all about them—what towns in the South they were from, and every detail of their connection with the conspiracy.

But they all denied his facts, and not one of them confessed a thing. The men raged, the women cried. According to their stories, they were all innocent people from out West, and loved the Union above all things in this world. I locked the gang up, in disgust, and fell to catechising Wicklow once more.

"Where is No. 166, and who is B. B.?"

But *there* he was determined to draw the line. Neither coaxing nor threats had any effect upon him. Time was flying—it was necessary to institute sharp measures. So I tied him up a-tiptoe by the thumbs. As the pain increased, it wrung screams from him which were almost more than I could bear. But I held my ground, and pretty soon he shrieked out,—

"Oh, *please* let me down, and I will tell!"

"No—you'll tell *before* I let you down."

Every instant was agony to him, now, so out it came,—

"No. 166, Eagle Hotel! "—naming a wretched tavern down by the water, a resort of common laborers, 'longshoremen, and less reputable folk.

So I released him, and then demanded to know the object of the conspiracy.

"To take the fort to-night," said he, doggedly and sobbing.

"Have I got all the chiefs of the conspiracy?"

"No. You've got all except those that are to meet at 166."

"What does 'Remember XXXX' mean?"

No reply.

"What is the password to No. 166?"

No reply.

"What do those bunches of letters mean,— 'FFFFF' and 'MMMM'? Answer! or you will catch it again."

"I never *will* answer! I will die first. Now do what you please."

"Think what you are saying, Wicklow. Is it final?"

He answered steadily, and without a quiver in his voice,—

"It is final.   As sure as I love my wronged country and hate everything this Northern sun shines on, I will die before I will reveal those things."

I triced him up by the thumbs again.   When the agony was full upon him, it was heartbreaking to hear the poor thing's shrieks, but we got nothing else out of him.   To every question he screamed the same reply: "I can die, and I *will* die; but I will never tell."

Well, we had to give it up.   We were convinced that he certainly would die rather than confess.   So we took him down and imprisoned him, under strict guard.

Then for some hours we busied ourselves with sending telegrams to the War Department, and with making preparations for a descent upon No. 166.

It was stirring times, that black and bitter night.   Things had leaked out, and the whole garrison was on the alert.   The sentinels were trebled, and nobody could move, outside or in,

without being brought to a stand with a mus-
ket levelled at his head.   However, Webb and
I were less concerned now than we had previously been, because of the fact that the conspiracy must necessarily be in a pretty crippled
condition, since so many of its principals were
in our clutches.

I determined to be at No. 166 in good season, capture and gag B. B., and be on hand
for the rest when they arrived.   At about a
quarter past one in the morning I crept out of
the fortress with half a dozen stalwart and
gamy U. S. regulars at my heels—and the boy
Wicklow, with his hands tied behind him.   I
told him we were going to No. 166, and that if
I found he had lied again and was misleading
us, he would have to show us the right place
or suffer the consequences.

We approached the tavern stealthily and
reconnoitred.   A light was burning in the
small bar-room, the rest of the house was
dark.   I tried the front door; it yielded, and
we softly entered, closing the door behind us.
Then we removed our shoes, and I led the

way to the bar-room. The German landlord
sat there, asleep in his chair. I woke him
gently, and told him to take off his boots and
precede us; warning him at the same time to
utter no sound. He obeyed without a mur-
mur, but evidently he was badly frightened.
I ordered him to lead the way to 166. We
ascended two or three flights of stairs as softly
as a file of cats; and then, having arrived near
the farther end of a long hall, we came to a
door through the glazed transom of which we
could discern the glow of a dim light from
within. The landlord felt for me in the dark
and whispered me that that was 166. I tried
the door—it was locked on the inside. I whispered an order to one of my biggest soldiers;
we set our ample shoulders to the door and
with one heave we burst it from its hinges. I
caught a half-glimpse of a figure in a bed—
saw its head dart toward the candle; out went
the light, and we were in pitch darkness.
With one big bound I lit on that bed and
pinned its occupant down with my knees. My
prisoner struggled fiercely, but I got a grip on

his throat with my left hand, and that was a good assistance to my knees in holding him down. Then straightway I snatched out my revolver, cocked it, and laid the cold barrel warningly against his cheek.

"Now somebody strike a light!" said I. "I've got him safe."

It was done. The flame of the match burst up. I looked at my captive, and, by George, it was a young woman!

I let go and got off the bed, feeling pretty sheepish. Everybody stared stupidly at his neighbor. Nobody had any wit or sense left, so sudden and overwhelming had been the surprise. The young woman began to cry, and covered her face with the sheet. The landlord said, meekly,—

"My daughter, she has been doing something that is not right, *nicht wahr?*"

"Your daughter? Is she your daughter?"

"Oh, yes, she is my daughter. She is just to-night come home from Cincinnati a little bit sick."

"Confound it, that boy has lied again. This

is not the right 166; this is not B. B. Now, Wicklow, you will find the correct 166 for us, or—hello! where is that boy?"

Gone, as sure as guns! And, what is more, we failed to find a trace of him. Here was an awkward predicament. I cursed my stupidity in not tying him to one of the men; but it was of no use to bother about that now. What should I do in the present circumstances?— that was the question. That girl *might* be B. B., after all. I did not believe it, but still it would not answer to take unbelief for proof. So I finally put my men in a vacant room across the hall from 166, and told them to capture anybody and everybody that approached the girl's room, and to keep the landlord with them, and under strict watch, until further orders. Then I hurried back to the fort to see if all was right there yet.

Yes, all was right. And all remained right. I stayed up all night to make sure of that. Nothing happened. I was unspeakably glad to see the dawn come again, and be able to telegraph the Department that the Stars and Stripes still floated over Fort Trumbull.

An immense pressure was lifted from my breast. Still I did not relax vigilance, of course, nor effort either; the case was too grave for that. I had up my prisoners, one by one, and harried them by the hour, trying to get them to confess, but it was a failure. They only gnashed their teeth and tore their hair, and revealed nothing.

About noon came tidings of my missing boy. He had been seen on the road, tramping westward, some eight miles out, at six in the morning. I started a cavalry lieutenant and a private on his track at once. They came in sight of him twenty miles out. He had climbed a fence and was wearily dragging himself across a slushy field toward a large old-fashioned mansion in the edge of a village. They rode through a bit of woods, made a detour, and closed up on the house from the opposite side; then dismounted and skurried into the kitchen. Nobody there. They slipped into the next room, which was also unoccupied; the door from that room into the front or sitting room was open. They were about to step through it when they heard a low voice; it was somebody praying. So they halted reverently, and the lieutenant put his head in and saw an old man and an old woman kneeling in a corner of that sitting-room. It was the old man that was praying, and just as he was finishing his prayer, the Wicklow boy opened the front door and stepped in. Both of those old people sprang at him and smothered him with embraces, shouting,—

"Our boy! our darling! God be praised. The lost is found! He that was dead is alive again!"

Well, sir, what do you think! That young imp was born and reared on that homestead, and had never been five miles away from it in all his life, till the fortnight before he loafed into my quarters and gulled me with that maudlin yarn of his! It's as true as gospel. That old man was his father—a learned old retired clergyman; and that old lady was his mother.

Let me throw in a word or two of explanation concerning that boy and his performances. It turned out that he was a ravenous devourer of dime novels and sensation-story papers— therefore, dark mysteries and gaudy heroisms were just in his line. Then he had read newspaper reports of the stealthy goings and comings of rebel spies in our midst, and of their lurid purposes and their two or three startling achievements, till his imagination was all aflame on that subject. His constant comrade for some months had been a Yankee youth of much tongue and lively fancy, who had served for a couple of years as "mud clerk" (that is, subordinate purser) on certain of the packet-boats plying between New Orleans and points two or three hundred miles up the Mississippi —hence his easy facility in handling the names and other details pertaining to that region. Now I had spent two or three months in that part of the country before the war; and I knew just enough about it to be easily taken in by that boy, whereas a born Louisianian would probably have caught him tripping before he had talked fifteen minutes.   Do you know the reason he said he would rather die than explain certain of his treasonable enigmas? Simply because he *could n't* explain them!— they had no meaning; he had fired them out of his imagination without forethought or afterthought; and so, upon sudden call, he was n't able to invent an explanation of them. For instance, he could n't reveal what was hidden in the "sympathetic ink" letter, for the ample reason that there was n't anything hidden in it; it was blank paper only. He had n't put anything into a gun, and had never intended to—for his letters were all written to imaginary persons, and when he hid one in the stable he always removed the one he had put there the day before; so he was not acquainted with that knotted string, since he was seeing it for the first time when I showed it to him; but as soon as I had let him find out where it came from, he straightway adopted it, in his romantic fashion, and got some fine effects out of it. He invented Mr. "Gaylord;" there was n't any 15 Bond Street, just then—it had been pulled down three months before. He invented the "Colonel;" he invented the glib histories of those unfortunates whom I captured and confronted with him; he invented "B. B.;" he even invented No. 166, one may say, for he did n't know there *was* such a number in the Eagle Hotel until we went there. He stood ready to invent anybody or anything whenever it was wanted. If I called for "outside" spies, he promptly described strangers whom he had seen at the hotel, and whose names he had happened to hear. Ah, he lived in a gorgeous, mysterious, romantic world during those few stirring days, and I think it was *real* to him, and that he enjoyed it clear down to the bottom of his heart.

But he made trouble enough for us, and just no end of humiliation. You see, on account of him we had fifteen or twenty people under arrest and confinement in the fort, with sentinels before their doors. A lot of the captives were soldiers and such, and to them I did n't have to apologize; but the rest were first-class citizens, from all over the country, and no amount of apologies was sufficient to satisfy them. They just fumed and raged and made no end of trouble! And those two ladies,—one was an Ohio Congressman's wife, the other a Western bishop's sister,—well, the scorn and ridicule and angry tears they poured out on me made up a keepsake that was likely to make me remember them for a considerable time,—and I shall. That old lame gentleman with the goggles was a college president from Philadelphia, who had come up to attend his nephew's funeral. He had never seen young Wicklow before, of course. Well, he not only missed the funeral, and got jailed as a rebel spy, but Wicklow had stood up there in my quarters and coldly described him as a counterfeiter, nigger-trader, horse-thief, and fire-bug from the most notorious rascal-nest in Galveston; and this was a thing which that poor old gentleman could n't seem to get over at all.

And the War Department! But, O my soul, let's draw the curtain over that part!

NOTE.—I showed my manuscript to the Major, and he said: "Your unfamiliarity with military matters has betrayed you into some little mistakes. Still, they are picturesque ones—let them go; military men will smile at them, the rest won't detect them. You have got the main facts of the history right, and have set them down just about as they occurred."—M. T.

MRS. McWILLIAMS AND THE LIGHTNING.

WELL, sir,—continued Mr. McWilliams, for this was not the beginning of his talk;—the fear of lightning is one of the most distressing infirmities a human being can be afflicted with. It is mostly confined to women; but now and then you find it in a little dog, and sometimes in a man. It is a particularly distressing infirmity, for the reason that it takes the sand out of a person to an extent which no other fear can, and it can't be *reasoned* with, and neither can it be shamed out of a person. A woman who could face the very devil himself—or a mouse—loses her grip and goes all to pieces in front of a flash of lightning. Her fright is something pitiful to see.

Well, as I was telling you, I woke up, with that smothered and unlocatable cry of " Mortimer ! Mortimer !" wailing in my ears ; and as soon as I could scrape my faculties together I reached over in the dark and then said,—

" Evangeline, is that you calling ? What is the matter ? Where are you ? "

" Shut up in the boot-closet. You ought to be ashamed to lie there and sleep so, and such an awful storm going on."

" Why, how *can* one be ashamed when he is asleep ? It is unreasonable ; a man *can't* be ashamed when he is asleep, Evangeline."

" You never try, Mortimer,—you know very well you never try."

I caught the sound of muffled sobs.

That sound smote dead the sharp speech that was on my lips, and I changed it to—

" I'm sorry, dear,—I'm truly sorry. I never meant to act so. Come back and—"

" MORTIMER ! "

" Heavens ! what is the matter, my love ? "

" Do you mean to say you are in that bed yet ? "

" Why, of course."

" Come out of it instantly. I should think

you would take some *little* care of your life, for *my* sake and the children's, if you will not for your own."

"But my love—"

"Don't talk to me, Mortimer. You *know* there is no place so dangerous as a bed, in such a thunder-storm as this,—all the books say that; yet there you would lie, and deliberately throw away your life, — for goodness knows what, unless for the sake of arguing and arguing, and—"

"But, confound it, Evangeline, I'm *not* in the bed, *now.* I'm—"

[Sentence interrupted by a sudden glare of lightning, followed by a terrified little scream from Mrs. McWilliams and a tremendous blast of thunder.]

"There! You see the result. Oh, Mortimer, how *can* you be so profligate as to swear at such a time as this?"

"I *didn't* swear. And that *was n't* a result of it, any way. It would have come, just the same, if I had n't said a word; and you know very well, Evangeline,—at least you ought to know,—that when the atmosphere is charged with electricity—"

"Oh, yes, now argue it, and argue it, and argue it!—I don't see how you can act so, when you *know* there is not a lightning-rod on the place, and your poor wife and children are absolutely at the mercy of Providence. What *are* you doing?—lighting a match at such a time as this! Are you stark mad?"

"Hang it, woman, where's the harm? The place is as dark as the inside of an infidel, and—"

"Put it out! put it out instantly! Are you determined to sacrifice us all? You *know* there is nothing attracts lightning like a light. [*Fzt! —crash! boom — boloom-boom-boom!*] Oh, just hear it! Now you see what you've done!"

"No, I *don't* see what I've done. A match may attract lightning, for all I know, but it don't *cause* lightning,—I'll go odds on that. And it didn't attract it worth a cent this time; for if that shot was levelled at my match, it was blessed poor marksmanship, — about an

average of none out of a possible million, I
should say. Why, at Dollymount, such marksmanship as that—"

"For shame, Mortimer! Here we are
standing right in the very presence of death,
and yet in so solemn a moment you are capable of using such language as that. If you
have no desire to—Mortimer!"

"Well?"

"Did you say your prayers to-night?"

"I—I—meant to, but I got to trying to
cipher out how much twelve times thirteen is,
and—"

[*Fzt!—boom-berroom-boom! bumble-umble
bang*-SMASH!]

"Oh, we are lost, beyond all help! How
could you neglect such a thing at such a time
as this?"

"But it *was n't* 'such a time as this.' There
was n't a cloud in the sky. How could *I* know
there was going to be all this rumpus and pow-
wow about a little slip like that? And I don't
think it's just fair for you to make so much out
of it, any way, seeing it happens so seldom; I

have n't missed before since I brought on that earthquake, four years ago."

"MORTIMER! How you talk! Have you forgotten the yellow fever?"

"My dear, you are always throwing up the yellow fever to me, and I think it is perfectly unreasonable. You can't even send a telegraphic message as far as Memphis without relays, so how is a little devotional slip of mine going to carry so far? I'll *stand* the earthquake, because it was in the neighborhood; but I'll be hanged if I'm going to be responsible for every blamed—"

[*Fzt !*— BOOM *beroom*-boom! boom!— BANG!]

"Oh, dear, dear, dear! I *know* it struck something, Mortimer. We never shall see the light of another day; and if it will do you any good to remember, when we are gone, that your dreadful language—*Mortimer!*"

"WELL! What now?"

"Your voice sounds as if— Mortimer, are you actually standing in front of that open fireplace?"

" That is the very crime I am committing."

" Get away from it, this moment. You do seem determined to bring destruction on us all. Don't you *know* that there is no better conductor for lightning than an open chimney? *Now* where have you got to ?"

" I'm here by the window."

" Oh, for pity's sake, have you lost your mind ? Clear out from there, this moment. The very children in arms know it is fatal to stand near a window in a thunder-storm. Dear, dear, I know I shall never see the light of another day. Mortimer ?"

" Yes ?"

" What is that rustling ?"

" It's me."

" What are you doing ?"

" Trying to find the upper end of my pantaloons."

" Quick ! throw those things away ! I do believe you would deliberately put on those clothes at such a time as this; yet you know perfectly well that *all* authorities agree that woolen stuffs attract lightning. Oh, dear,

dear, it isn't sufficient that one's life must be in peril from natural causes, but you must do everything you can possibly think of to augment the danger. Oh, *don't* sing! What *can* you be thinking of?"

"Now where's the harm in it?"

"Mortimer, if I have told you once, I have told you a hundred times, that singing causes vibrations in the atmosphere which interrupt the flow of the electric fluid, and— What on *earth* are you opening that door for?"

"Goodness gracious, woman, is there is any harm in *that?*"

"*Harm?* There's *death* in it. Anybody that has given this subject any attention knows that to create a draught is to invite the lightning. You have n't half shut it; shut it *tight*, —and do hurry, or we are all destroyed. Oh, it is an awful thing to be shut up with a lunatic at such a time as this. Mortimer, what *are* you doing?"

"Nothing. Just turning on the water. This room is smothering hot and close. I want to bathe my face and hands."

"You have certainly parted with the remnant of your mind! Where lightning strikes any other substance once, it strikes water fifty times. Do turn it off. Oh, dear, I am sure that nothing in this world can save us. It does seem to me that— Mortimer, what was that?"

"It was a da— it was a picture. Knocked it down."

"Then you are close to the wall! I never heard of such imprudence! Don't you *know* that there's no better conductor for lightning than a wall? Come away from there! And you came as near as anything to swearing, too. Oh, how can you be so desperately wicked, and your family in such peril? Mortimer, did you order a feather bed, as I asked you to do?"

"No. Forgot it."

"Forgot it! It may cost you your life. If you had a feather bed, now, and could spread it in the middle of the room and lie on it, you would be perfectly safe. Come in here,— come quick, before you have a chance to commit any more frantic indiscretions."

I tried, but the little closet would not hold us both with the door shut, unless we could be content to smother. I gasped awhile, then forced my way out. My wife called out,—

" Mortimer, something *must* be done for your preservation. Give me that German book that is on the end of the mantel-piece, and a candle; but don't light it; give me a match; I will light it in here. That book has some directions in it."

I got the book,—at cost of a vase and some other brittle things; and the madam shut herself up with her candle. I had a moment's peace; then she called out,—

" Mortimer, what was that?"

" Nothing but the cat."

" The cat! Oh, destruction! Catch her, and shut her up in the wash-stand. Do be quick, love; cats are *full* of electricity. I just know my hair will turn white with this night's awful perils."

I heard the muffled sobbings again. But for that, I should not have moved hand or foot in such a wild enterprise in the dark.

However, I went at my task,—over chairs, and against all sorts of obstructions, all of them hard ones, too, and most of them with sharp edges,—and at last I got kitty cooped up in the commode, at an expense of over four hundred dollars in broken furniture and shins. Then these muffled words came from the closet:—

"It says the safest thing is to stand on a chair in the middle of the room, Mortimer; and the legs of the chair must be insulated, with non-conductors. That is, you must set the legs of the chair in glass tumblers. [*Fzt !— boom—bang !—smash !*] Oh, hear that ! Do hurry, Mortimer, before you are struck."

I managed to find and secure the tumblers. I got the last four,—broke all the rest. I insulated the chair legs, and called for further instructions.

"Mortimer, it says, 'Während eines Gewitters entferne man Metalle, wie z. B., Ringe, Uhren, Schlüssel, etc., von sich und halte sich auch nicht an solchen Stellen auf, wo viele Metalle bei einander liegen, oder mit andern

Körpern verbunden sind, wie an Herden,
Oefen, Eisengittern u. dgl.' What does that
mean, Mortimer ? Does it mean that you
must keep metals *about* you, or keep them *away*
from you ? "

" Well, I hardly know. It appears to be a
little mixed. All German advice is more or
less mixed. However, I think that that sentence is mostly in the dative case, with a little
genitive and accusative sifted in, here and
there, for luck ; so I reckon it means that you
must keep some metals *about* you."

" Yes, that must be it. It stands to reason
that it is. They are in the nature of lightning-
rods, you know. Put on your fireman's hel-
met, Mortimer ; that is mostly metal."

I got it and put it on,—a very heavy and
clumsy and uncomfortable thing on a hot night
in a close room. Even my night-dress seemed
to be more clothing than I strictly needed.

" Mortimer, I think your middle ought to be
protected. Won't you buckle on your militia
sabre, please ? "

I complied.

"Now, Mortimer, you ought to have some way to protect your feet. Do please put on your spurs."

I did it,—in silence,—and kept my temper as well as I could.

"Mortimer, it says, ' Das Gewitter läuten ist sehr gefährlich, weil die Glocke selbst, sowie der durch das Läuten veranlasste Luftzug und die Höhe des Thurmes den Blitz anziehen könnten.' Mortimer, does that mean that it is dangerous not to ring the church bells during a thunder-storm?"

"Yes, it seems to mean that,—if that is the past participle of the nominative case singular, and I reckon it is. Yes, I think it means that on account of the height of the church tower and the absence of *Luftzug* it would be very dangerous (*sehr gefährlich*) not to ring the bells in time of a storm; and moreover, don't you see, the very wording—"

"Never mind that, Mortimer ; don't waste the precious time in talk. Get the large dinner-bell ; it is right there in the hall. Quick, Mortimer dear ; we are almost safe. Oh, dear,

I do believe we are going to be saved, at last!"

Our little summer establishment stands on top of a high range of hills, overlooking a valley. Several farm-houses are in our neighborhood,—the nearest some three or four hundred yards away.

When I, mounted on the chair, had been clanging that dreadful bell a matter of seven or eight minutes, our shutters were suddenly torn open from without, and a brilliant bull's-eye lantern was thrust in at the window, followed by a hoarse inquiry :—

" What in the nation is the matter here ? "

The window was full of men's heads, and the heads were full of eyes that stared wildly at my night-dress and my warlike accoutrements.

I dropped the bell, skipped down from the chair in confusion, and said,—

" There is nothing the matter, friends,—only a little discomfort on account of the thunder-storm. I was trying to keep off the lightning."

" Thunder-storm ? Lightning ? Why, Mr. McWilliams, have you lost your mind ? It is a beautiful starlight night ; there has been no storm."

I looked out, and I was so astonished I could hardly speak for a while. Then I said,—

" I do not understand this. We distinctly saw the glow of the flashes through the curtains and shutters, and heard the thunder."

One after another of those people lay down on the ground to laugh,—and two of them died. One of the survivors remarked,—

" Pity you did n't think to open your blinds and look over to the top of the high hill yonder. What you heard was cannon ; what you saw was the flash. You see, the telegraph brought some news, just at midnight : Garfield's nominated,—and that's what's the matter !"

Yes, Mr. Twain, as I was saying in the beginning (said Mr. McWilliams), the rules for preserving people against lightning are so excellent and so innumerable that the most incomprehensible thing in the world to me is how anybody ever manages to get struck.

So saying, he gathered up his satchel and umbrella, and departed ; for the train had reached his town.

[EXPLANATORY. I regard the idea of this play as a valuable invention. I call it the Patent Universally-Applicable Automatically-Adjustable Language Drama. This indicates that it is adjustable to any tongue, and performable in any tongue. The English portions of the play are to remain just as they are, permanently; but you change the foreign portions to any language you please, at will. Do you see? You at once have the same old play in a new tongue. And you can keep on changing it from language to language, until your private theatrical pupils have become glib and at home in the speech of all nations. *Zum Beispiel*, suppose we wish to adjust the play to the French tongue. First, we give Mrs. Blumenthal and Gretchen French names. Next, we knock the German Meisterschaft sentences out of the first scene, and replace them with sentences from the French Meisterschaft—like this, for instance; " Je voudrais faire des emplettes ce matin; voulez-vous avoir l'obligeance de venir avec moi chez le tailleur français?" And so on. Wherever you find German, replace it with French, leaving the English parts undisturbed. When you come to the long conversation in the second act, turn to any pamphlet of your French Meisterschaft, and shovel in as much French talk on *any* subject as will fill up the gaps left by the expunged German. Example—page 423 French Meisterschaft:

On dirait qu'il va faire chaud.
J'ai chaud.
J'ai extrêmement chaud.
Ah! qu'il fait chaud!
Il fait une chaleur étouffante!
L'air est brûlant.
Je meurs de chaleur.
Il est presque impossible de supporter la chaleur.
Cela vous fait transpirer.
Mettons nous à l'ombre.
Il fait du vent.
Il fait un vent froid.
Il fait un temps très-agréable pour se promener aujour-
    d'hui.

And so on, all the way through. It is very easy to adjust the play to any desired language. Anybody can do it.]

MEISTERSCHAFT: IN THREE ACTS.

DRAMATIS PERSONÆ:

Mr. Stephenson.   Margaret Stephenson.
George Franklin.   Annie Stephenson.
William Jackson.   Mrs. Blumenthal, the Wirthin.
            Gretchen, Kellnerin.

ACT I.

SCENE I.

Scene of the play, the parlor of a small private dwelling in a village.

Margaret. (*Discovered crocheting — has a pamphlet.*)

Margaret. (*Solus.*) Dear, dear! it's dreary enough, to have to study this impossible German tongue : to be exiled from home and all human society except a body's sister in order to do it, is just simply abscheulich. Here's only three weeks of the three months gone, and it seems like three years. I don't believe I can live through it, and I'm sure Annie can't. (*Refers to her book, and rattles through, sev-*

eral times, like one memorizing:) Entschuldigen Sie, mein Herr, können Sie mir vielleicht
sagen, um wie viel Uhr der erste Zug nach
Dresden abgeht? (*Makes mistakes and cor-
rects them.*) I just hate Meisterschaft! We
may see people; we can have society: yes,
on condition that the conversation shall be in
German, and in German only—every single
word of it! Very kind—oh, very! when
neither Annie nor I can put two words together, except as they are put together for us in
Meisterschaft or that idiotic Ollendorff! (*Refers to book, and memorizes: Mein Bruder hat
Ihren Herrn Vater nicht gesehen, als er gestern
in dem Laden des deutschen Kaufmannes war.*)
Yes, we can have society, provided we talk
German. What would such a conversation be
like! If you should stick to Meisterschaft, it
would change the subject every two minutes;
and if you stuck to Ollendorff, it would be all
about your sister's mother's good stocking of
thread, or your grandfather's aunt's good hammer of the carpenter, and who's got it, and
there an end. You couldn't keep up your in-

terest in such topics. (*Memorizing: Wenn irgend möglich,—möchte ich noch heute Vormittag dort ankommen, da es mir sehr daran gelegen ist, einen meiner Geschäftsfreunde zu treffen.*) My mind is made up to one thing: I will be an exile, in spirit and in truth: I will see no one during these three months. Father is very ingenious—oh, very! thinks he is, anyway. Thinks he has invented a way to *force* us to learn to speak German. He is a dear good soul, and all that; but invention isn't his fash'. He will see. (*With eloquent energy.*) Why, nothing in the world shall—Bitte, können Sie mir vielleicht sagen, ob Herr Schmidt mit diesem Zuge angekommen ist? Oh, dear, dear George—three weeks! It seems a whole century since I saw him. I wonder if he suspects that I—that I—care for him——j—just a wee, wee bit? I believe he does. And I believe Will suspects that Annie cares for *him* a little, that I do. And I know perfectly well that they care for *us*. They agree with all our opinions, no matter what they are; and if they have a prejudice, they change it, as soon as they see how foolish it is. Dear George! at first he just couldn't abide cats; but now, why now he's just all for cats; he fairly welters in cats. I never saw such a reform. And it's just so with *all* his principles: he hasn't got one that he had before. Ah, if all men were like him, this world would——(*Memorizing : Im Gegentheil, mein Herr, dieser Stoff is sehr billig. Bitte, sehen Sie sich nur die Qualität an.*) Yes, and what did *they* go to studying German for, if it wasn't an inspiration of the highest and purest sympathy? Any other explanation is nonsense——why, they'd as soon have thought of studying American history. (*Turns her back, buries herself in her pamphlet, first memorizing aloud, until Annie enters, then to herself, rocking to and fro, and rapidly moving her lips, without uttering a sound.*)

Enter Annie, absorbed in her pamphlet—does not at first see Margaret.

ANNIE. (*Memorizing : Er liess mich ges-tern früh rufen, und sagte mir dass er einen sehr unangenehmen Brief von Ihrem Lehrer erhalten hatte. Repeats twice aloud, then to herself, briskly moving her lips.*)

M. (*Still not seeing her sister.*) Wie geht es Ihrem Herrn Schwiegervater? Es freut mich sehr dass Ihre Frau Mutter wieder wohl ist. (*Repeats. Then mouths in silence.*)

(*Annie repeats her sentence a couple of times aloud; then looks up, working her lips, and discovers Margaret.*) Oh, you here! (*Running to her.*) O lovey-dovey, dovey-lovey, I've got the gr-reatest news! Guess, guess, guess! You'll never guess in a hundred thousand million years—and more!

M. Oh, tell me, tell me, dearie; don't keep me in agony.

A. Well, I will. What—do—you—think? *They're* here!

M. Wh-a-t! Who? When? Which? Speak!

A. Will and George!

M. Annie Alexandra Victoria Stephenson, what *do* you mean!

A. As sure as guns!

M. (*Spasmodically unarming and kissing*

her.) 'Sh! don't use such language. O darling, say it again!

A. As sure as guns!

M. I don't mean that! Tell me again,
that—

A. (*Springing up and waltzing about the
room*.) They're here—in this very village—to
learn German—for three months! Es sollte
mich sehr freuen wenn Sie—

M. (*Joining in the dance*.) Oh, it's just too
lovely for anything! (*Unconsciously memorizing :*) Es wäre mir lieb wenn Sie morgen mit
mir in die Kirche gehen könnten, aber ich kann
selbst nicht gehen, weil ich Sonntags gewöhn-
lich krank bin. Juckhe!

A. (*Finishing some unconscious memorizing.*)—morgen Mittag bei mir speisen könnten.
Juckhe! Sit down and I'll tell you all I've
heard. (*They sit.*) They're here, and under
that same odious law that fetters us—our
tongues, I mean; the metaphor's faulty, but no
matter. They can go out, and see people, only
on condition that they hear and speak German, and German only.

M. Isn't—that—too lovely!

A. And they're coming to see us!

M. Darling! (*Kissing her.*) But are you sure?

A. Sure as guns—Gatling guns!

M. 'Sh! don't child, it's schrecklich! Darling—you aren't mistaken?

A. As sure as g—batteries!

They jump up and dance a moment—then—

M. (*With distress.*) But, Annie dear!—*we* can't talk German—and neither can they!

A. (*Sorrowfully.*) I didn't think of that.

M. How cruel it is! What can we do?

A. (*After a reflective pause, resolutely.*) Margaret—we've *got* to.

M. Got to what?

A. Speak German.

M. Why, how, child?

A. (*Contemplating her pamphlet with earnestness.*) I can tell you one thing. Just give me the blessed privilege: just hinsetzen Will Jackson here in front of me and I'll talk German to him as long as this Meisterschaft holds out to burn.

M. (*Joyously.*)   Oh, what an elegant idea !
You certainly have got a mind that's a mine of
resources, if ever anybody had one.

A. I'll skin this Meisterschaft to the last sentence in it !

M. (*With a happy idea.*)   Why, Annie, it's
the greatest thing in the world.   I've been all
this time struggling and despairing over these
few little Meisterschaft primers: but as sure as
you live, I'll have the whole fifteen by heart
before this time day after to-morrow.   See if I
don't.

A. And so will I; and I'll trowel-in a layer
of Ollendorff mush between every couple of
courses of Meisterschaft bricks.   Juckhe !

M. Hoch ! hoch ! hoch !

A. Stoss an !

M. Juckhe !   Wir   werden   gleich   gute
deutsche Schülerinnen werden !   Juck——

A. —he !

M. Annie, when are they coming to see us ?
To-night ?

A. No.

M. No? Why not? When are they coming ?

What are they waiting for ? The idea ! I never heard of such a thing ! What do you——

A. (*Breaking in.*) Wait, wait, wait ! give a body a chance. They have their reasons.

M. Reasons ?—what reasons ?

A. Well, now, when you stop and think, they're royal good ones. They've got to talk German when they come, haven't they ? Of course. Well, they don't *know* any German but Wie befinden Sie sich, and Haben Sie gut geschlafen, and Vater unser, and Ich trinke lieber Bier als Wasser, and a few little parlor things like that; but when it comes to *talking*, why, they don't know a hundred and fifty German words, put them all together.

M. Oh, I see !

A. So they're going neither to eat, sleep, smoke, nor speak the truth till they've crammed home the whole fifteen Meisterschafts auswendig !

M. Noble hearts !

A. They've given themselves till day after to-morrow, half-past 7 P. M., and then they'll arrive here, loaded.

M. Oh, how lovely, how gorgeous, how beautiful ! Some think this world is made of mud; I think it's made of rainbows. (*Memorizing.*) Wenn irgend möglich, so möchte ich noch heute Vormittag dort ankommen, da es mir sehr daran gelegen ist,—Annie, I can learn it just like nothing !

A. So can I. Meisterschaft's mere fun—I don't see how it ever could have seemed difficult. Come ! We can be disturbed here: let's give orders that we don't want anything to eat for two days; and are absent to friends, dead to strangers, and not at home even to nougat-peddlers——

M. Schön ! and we'll lock ourselves into our rooms, and at the end of two days, whosoever may ask us a Meisterschaft question shall get a Meisterschaft answer — and hot from the bat !

BOTH. (*Reciting in unison.*) Ich habe einen Hut für meinen Sohn, ein Paar Handschuhe für meinen Bruder, und einen Kamm für mich selbst gekauft.

(Exeunt.)

Enter Mrs. Blumenthal, the Wirthin.

WIRTHIN. (*Solus.*) Ach, die armen Mädchen, sie hassen die deutsche Sprache, drum ist es ganz und gar unmöglich dass sie sie je lernen können. Es bricht mir ja mein Herz ihre Kummer über die Studien anzusehen . . . . Warum haben sie den Entchluss gefasst in ihren Zimmern ein Paar Tage zu bleiben? . . . Ja—gewiss—dass versteht sich: sie sind entmuthigt—arme Kinder!

(*A knock at the door.*) Herein!
Enter Gretchen with card.

G. Er ist schon wieder da, und sagt dass er nur *Sie* sehen will. (*Hands the card.*) Auch—

WIRTHIN. Gott im Himmel—der Vater der Mädchen! (*Puts the card in her pocket.*) Er wünscht die *Töchter* nicht zu treffen? Ganz recht; also, Du schweigst.

G. Zu Befehl.

WIRTHIN. Lass ihn hereinkommen.

G. Ja, Frau Wirthin!
Exit Gretchen.

WIRTHIN. (*Solus.*) Ah—jetzt muss ich ihm die Wahrheit offenbaren.

Enter Mr. Stephenson.

STEPHENSON. Good morning, Mrs. Blumenthal—keep your seat, keep your seat, please.
I'm only here for a moment—merely to get
your report, you know. (*Seating himself.*)
Don't want to see the girls—poor things,
they'd want to go home with me. I'm afraid
I couldn't have the heart to say no. How's
the German getting along ?

WIRTHIN. N-not very well; I was afraid you
would ask me that. You see, they hate it, they
don't take the least interest in it, and there
isn't anything to incite them to an interest, you
see. And so they can't talk at all.

S. M-m. That's bad. I had an idea that
they'd get lonesome, and have to seek society;
and then, of course, my plan would work, considering the cast-iron conditions of it.

WIRTHIN. But it hasn't so far. I've thrown
nice company in their way—I've done my very
best, in every way I could think of—but it's no
use; they won't go out, and they won't receive
anybody. And a body can't blame them;
they'd be tongue-tied—couldn't do anything

with a German conversation. Now when I started to learn German—such poor German as I know—the case was very different: my intended was a German. I was to live among Germans the rest of my life; and so I *had* to learn. Why, bless my heart ! I nearly *lost* the man the first time he asked me—I thought he was talking about the measles. They were very prevalent at the time. Told him I didn't want any in mine. But I found out the mistake, and I was fixed for him next time. . . Oh, yes, Mr. Stephenson, a sweetheart's a prime incentive !

S. (*Aside.*) Good soul ! she doesn't suspect that my plan is a double scheme—includes a speaking knowledge of German, which I am bound they shall have, and the keeping them away from those two young fellows—though if I had known that those boys were going off for a year's foreign travel, I—however, the girls would never learn that language at home; they're here, and I won't relent—they've got to stick the three months out. (*Aloud.*) So they are making poor progress ? Now tell

me—will they learn it—after a sort of fashion,
I mean—in the three months ?

WIRTHIN. Well, now, I'll tell you the only
chance I see.   Do what I will, they won't answer my German with anything but English;
if that goes on, they'll stand stock still.   Now
I'm willing to do this: I'll straighten everything up, get matters in smooth running order,
and day after to-morrow I'll go to bed sick, and
stay sick three weeks.

S. Good !   You are an angel ! I see your
idea.   The servant girl—

WIRTHIN. That's it; that's my project. She
doesn't know a word of English.   And Gretchen's a real good soul, and can talk the slates
off a roof.   Her tongue's just a flutter-mill. I'll
keep my room,—just ailing a little,—and
they'll never see my face except when they pay
their little duty-visits to me, and then I'll say
English disorders my mind.   They'll be shut
up with Gretchen's wind-mill, and she'll just
grind them to powder.   Oh, *they'll* get a start
in the language—sort of a one, sure's you live.
You come back in three weeks.

S. Bless you, my Retterin ! I'll be here to
the day ! Get ye to your sick-room—you
shall have treble pay. (*Looking at watch.*)
Good ! I can just catch my train. Leben Sie
wohl ! (*Exit.*)

WIRTHIN. Leben Sie wohl ! mein Herr !

ACT II.

SCENE I.

Time, a couple of days later.
(The girls discovered with their work and primers.)

ANNIE. Was fehlt der Wirthin ?

MARGARET. Dass weiss ich nicht. Sie ist
schon vor zwei Tagen ins Bett gegangen—

A. My ! how fleissend you speak !

M. Danke schön—und sagte dass sie nicht
wohl sei.

A. Good ! Oh, no, I don't mean that ! no
—only lucky for *us*—glücklich, you know I
mean because it'll be so much nicer to have
them all to ourselves.

M. Oh, natürlich ! Ja ! Dass ziehe ich

durchaus vor.   Do you believe your Meisterschaft will stay with you, Annie?

A. Well, I know it *is* with me—every last
sentence of it; and a couple of hods of Ollendorff, too, for emergencies.   May be they'll refuse to deliver,—right off—at first, you know—
der Verlegenheit wegen—aber ich will sie spä-
ter herausholen—when I get my hand in—und
vergisst Du dass nicht!

M. Sei nicht grob, Liebste.   What shall we
talk about first—when they come?

A. Well—let me see.   There's shopping
—and—all that about the trains, you know,—
and going to church—and—buying tickets to
London, and Berlin, and all around—and all
that subjunctive stuff about the battle in Af-
ghanistan, and where the American was said
to be born, and so on—and—and ah—oh,
there's so *many* things—I don't think a body
can choose beforehand, because you know the
circumstances and the atmosphere always have
so much to do in directing a conversation, especially a German conversation, which is only
a kind of an insurrection, any way.   I believe

it's best to just depend on Prov—(*Glancing at watch, and gasping*)—half past—seven!

M. Oh, dear, I'm all of a tremble! Let's get something ready, Annie!

(*Both fall nervously to reciting*) : Entschuldigen Sie, mein Herr, können Sie mir vielleicht sagen wie ich nach dem norddeutchen Bahnhof gehe? (*They repeat it several times, losing their grip and mixing it all up.*)

(A knock.)

BOTH. Herein! Oh, dear! O der heilige—

Enter Gretchen.

GRETCHEN (*Ruffled and indignant.*) Entschuldigen Sie, meine gnädigsten Fräulein, es sind zwei junge rasende Herren draussen, die herein wollen, aber ich habe ihnen geschworen dass—(*Handing the cards.*)

M. Du liebe Zeit, they're here! And of course down goes my back hair! Stay and receive them, dear, while I—(*Leaving.*)

A. I—alone? I won't! I'll go with you! (*To* G.) Lass en Sie die Herren näher treten;

und sagen Sie ihnen dass wir gleich zurück-
kommen werden. (*Exit*.)

GR. (*Solus*.) Was! Sie freuen sich darüber?
Und ich sollte wirklich diese Blödsinnigen, dies
grobe Rindvieh hereinlassen? In den hülflosen
Umständen meiner gnädigen jungen Damen?
—Unsinn! (*Pause—thinking*.) Wohlan! Ich
werde sie mal beschützen! Sollte man nicht
glauben, dass sie einen Sparren zu viel hätten?
(*Tapping her skull significantly*.) Was sie mir
doch Alles gesagt haben! Der Eine: Guten
Morgen! wie geht es Ihrem Herrn Schwiegervater? Du liebe Zeit! Wie sollte ich einen
Schwiegervater haben können! Und der An-
dere: "Es thut mir sehr leid dass Ihrer Herr
Vater meinen Bruder nicht gesehen hat, als er
doch gestern in dem Laden des deutschen
Kaufmannes war!" Potztausendhimmelsdon-
nerwetter! Oh, ich war ganz rasend! Wie ich
aber rief: "Meine Herren, ich kenne Sie nicht,
und Sie kennen meinen Vater nicht, wissen Sie,
denn er ist schon lange durchgebrannt, und
geht nicht beim Tage in einen Laden hinein,
wissen Sie,—und ich habe keinen Schwieger-

vater, Gott sei Dank, werde auch nie einen kriegen, werde ueberhaupt, wissen Sie, ein solches Ding nie haben, nie dulden, nie ausstehen: warum greifen Sie ein Mädchen an, das nur Unschuld kennt, das Ihnen nie Etwas zu Leide gethan hat?" Dann haben sie sich beide die Finger in die Ohren gesteckt und gebetet : " Allmächtiger Gott ! Erbarme Dich unser !" (*Pauses*.) Nun, ich werde schon diesen Schurken Einlass gönnen, aber ich werde ein Auge mit ihnen haben, damit sie sich nicht wie reine Teufel geberden sollen.

(*Exit, grumbling and shaking her head.*)

Enter William and George.

W. My land, what a girl ! and what an incredible gift of gabble !—kind of patent climate-proof compensation-balance self-acting automatic Meisterschaft—touch her button, and br-r-r ! away she goes !

GEO. Never heard anything like it; tongue journaled on ball-bearings ! I wonder what she said; seemed to be swearing, mainly.

W. (*After mumbling Meisterschaft awhile.*)

Look here, George, this is awful—come to think—this project: *we* can't talk this frantic language.

GEO. I know it, Will, and it *is* awful; but I can't live without seeing Margaret—I've endured it as long as I can. I should die if I tried to hold out longer—and even German is preferable to death.

W. (*Hesitatingly.*)   Well, I don't know; it 's a matter of opinion.

GEO. (*Irritably.*)   It is n't a matter of opinion either.   German *is* preferable to death.

W. (*Reflectively.*)   Well, I don't know—the problem is so sudden—but I think you may be right: some kinds of death. It is more than likely that a slow, lingering—well, now, there in Canada in the early times a couple of centuries ago, the Indians would take a missionary and skin him, and get some hot ashes and boiling water and one thing and another, and by and by, that missionary—well, yes, I can see that, by and by, talking German could be a pleasant change for him.

GEO. Why, of course.   Das versteht sich;

but *you* have to always think a thing out, or you're not satisfied. But let's not go to bothering about thinking out this present business; we're here, we're in for it; you are as moribund to see Annie as I am to see Margaret; you know the terms: we've got to speak German. Now stop your mooning and get at your Meisterschaft; we've got nothing else in the world.

W. Do you think that 'll see us through?

GEO. Why it's *got* to. Suppose we wandered out of it and took a chance at the language on our own responsibility, where the nation would we be? Up a stump, that's where. Our only safety is in sticking like wax to the text.

W. But what can we talk about?

GEO. Why, anything that Meisterschaft talks about. It ain't our affair.

W. I know; but Meisterschaft talks about everything.

GEO. And yet don't talk about anything long enough for it to get embarrassing. Meisterschaft is just splendid for general conversation.

W. Yes, that's so; but it's so *blamed* general! Won't it sound foolish?

GEO. Foolish? Why, of course; all German sounds foolish.

W. Well, that is true; I didn't think of that.

GEO. Now, don't fool around any more. Load up; load up; get ready. Fix up some sentences; you'll need them in two minutes now.

(*They walk up and down, moving their lips in dumb-show memorizing.*)

W. Look here—when we've said all that's in the book on a topic, and want to change the subject, how can we say so?—how would a German say it?

GEO. Well, I don't know. But you know when they mean "Change cars," they say *Umsteigen*. Don't you reckon that will answer?

W. Tip-top! It's short and goes right to the point; and it's got a business whang to it that's almost American. Umsteigen!—change subject!—why, it's the very thing.

GEO. All right, then, *you* umsteigen—for I hear them coming.

Enter the girls.

A. TO W. (*With solemnity.*) Guten morgen, mein Herr, es freut mich sehr, Sie zu sehen.

W. Guten morgen, mein Fräulein, es freut mich sehr Sie zu sehen.

(*Margaret and George repeat the same sentences. Then, after an embarrassing silence, Margaret refers to her book and says:*)

M. Bitte, meine Herren, setzen Sie sich.

THE GENTLEMEN. Danke schön. (*The four seat themselves in couples, the width of the stage apart, and the two conversations begin. The talk is not flowing—at any rate at first; there are painful silences all along. Each couple worry out a remark and a reply: there is a pause of silent thinking, and then the other couple deliver themselves.*)

W. Haben Sie meinen Vater in dem Laden meines Bruders nicht gesehen?

A. Nein, mein Herr, ich habe Ihren Herrn Vater in dem Laden Ihres Herrn Bruders nicht gesehen.

GEO. Waren Sie gestern Abend im Koncert, oder im Theater?

M. Nein, ich war gestern Abend nicht im Koncert, noch im Theater, ich war gestern Abend zu Hause.

General break-down—long pause.

W. Ich störe doch nicht etwa?

A. Sie stören mich durchaus nicht.

GEO. Bitte, lassen Sie sich nicht von mir stören.

M. Aber ich bitte Sie, Sie stören mich durchaus nicht.

W. (*To both girls.*)   Wen wir Sie stören so gehen wir gleich wieder.

A. O, nein!   Gewiss, nein!

M. Im Gegentheil, es freut uns sehr, Sie zu sehen—alle Beide.

W. Schön!

GEO. Gott sei dank!

M. (*Aside.*)   It's just lovely!

A. (*Aside.*)   It's like a poem.

Pause.

W. Umsteigen!

M. Um—welches?

W. Umsteigen.

GEO. Auf English, change cars—oder subject.

BOTH GIRLS. Wie schön!

W. Wir haben uns die Freiheit genommen, bei Ihnen vorzusprechen.

A. Sie sind sehr gütig.

GEO. Wir wollten uns erkundigen, wie Sie sich befänden.

M. Ich bin Ihnen sehr verbunden—meine Schwester auch.

W. Meine Frau lasst sich Ihnen bestens empfehlen.

A. Ihre *Frau*?

W. (*Examining his book.*)   Vielleicht habe ich mich geirrt.   (*Shows the place.*) Nein, gerade so sagt das Buch.

A. (*Satisfied.*) Ganz recht.   Aber—

W. Bitte empfehlen Sie mich Ihrem Herrn Bruder.

A. Ah, dass ist viel besser—viel besser. (*Aside.*) Wenigstens es wäre viel besser wenn ich einen Bruder hätte.

GEO. Wie ist es Ihnen gegangen, seitdem ich das Vergnügen hätte, Sie anderswo zu sehen?

M. Danke bestens, ich befinde mich ge-
wöhnlich ziemlich wohl.

Gretchen slips in with a gun, and listens.

GEO. (*Still to Margaret.*) Befindet sich
Ihre Frau Gemahlin wohl?

GR. (*Raising hands and eyes.*) *Frau Gemahlin*—heiliger Gott! (*Is like to betray herself with her smothered laughter and glides
out.*)

M. Danke sehr, meine Frau ist ganz wohl.

Pause.

W. Dürfen wir vielleicht—umsteigen?

THE OTHERS. Gut!

GEO. (*Aside.*) I feel better, now. I'm beginning to catch on. (*Aloud.*) Ich mochte
gern morgen früh einige Einkäufe machen
und würde Ihnen sehr verbunden sein, wenn
Sie mir den Gefallen thäten, mir die Namen
der besten hiesigen Firmen aufzuschreiben.

M. (*Aside.*) How sweet!

W. (*Aside.*) Hang it, *I* was going to say
that! That's one of the noblest things in the
book.

A. Ich möchte Ihnen gern begleiten, aber es ist mir wirklich heute Morgen ganz unmöglich auszugehen. (*Aside.*) It's getting as easy as 9 times 7 is 46.

M. Sagen Sie dem Brieftäger, wenn's gefällig ist, er möchte Ihnen den ein geschriebenen Brief geben lassen.

W. Ich würde Ihnen sehr verbunden sein, wenn Sie diese Schachtel für mich nach der Post tragen würden, da mir sehr daran liegt einen meiner Geschäftsfreunde in dem Laden des deutchen Kaufmanns heute Abend treffen zu können. (*Aside.*) All down but nine; set 'm up on the other alley !

A. Aber Herr Jackson! Sie haben die Sätze gemischt. Es ist unbegreiflich wie Sie das haben thun können. Zwischen Ihrem ersten Theil und Ihrem letzten Theil haben Sie ganze fünfzig Seiten übergeschlagen ! Jetzt bin ich ganz verloren. Wie kann man reden, wenn man seinen Platz durchaus nicht wieder finden kann ?

W. Oh, bitte, verzeihen Sie; ich habe dass wirklich nich beabsichtigt.

A. (*Mollified.*) Sehr wohl, lassen Sie gut sein. Aber thun Sie es nicht wieder. Sie müssen ja doch einräumen, dass solche Dinge unerträgliche Verwirrung mit sich führen.

(*Gretchen slips in again with her gun.*)

W. Unzweifelhaft haben Sie Recht, meine holdselige Landsmännin. . . . . Umsteigen!

(As George gets fairly into the following, Gretchen draws a bead on him, and lets drive at the close, but the gun snaps.)

GEO. Glauben Sie dass ich ein hübsches Wohnzimmer für mich selbst und ein kleines Schlafzimmer für meinen Sohn in diesem Hotel für fünfzehn Mark die Woche bekommen kann, oder würden Sie mir rathen, in einer Privatwohnung Logis zu nehmen? (*Aside.*) That's a daisy!

GR. (*Aside.*) Schade! (*She draws her charge and reloads.*)

M. Glauben Sie nicht Sie werden besser thun bei diesem Wetter zu Hause zu bleiben?

A. Freilich glaube ich, Herr Franklin, Sie werden sich erkälten, wenn Sie bei diesem

unbeständigen Wetter ohne Ueberrock ausgehen.

GR. (*Relieved—aside.*) So ? Man redet von
Ausgehen. Das klingt schon besser. (*Sits.*)

W. (*To A.*) Wie theuer haben Sie das gekauft ? (*Indicating a part of her dress.*)

A. Das hat achtzehn Mark gekostet.

W. Das ist sehr theuer.

GEO. Ja, obgleich dieser Stoff wunderschön
ist und das Muster sehr geschmackvoll und
auch das Vorzüglichste dass es in dieser Art
gibt, so ist es doch furchtbar theuer für einen
solchen Artikel.

M. (*Aside.*) How sweet is this communion
of soul with soul !

A. Im Gegentheil, mein Herr, das ist sehr
billig. Sehen Sie sich nur die Qualität an.

(*They all examine it.*)

GEO. Möglicherweise ist es das allerneuste
dass man in diesem Stoff hat; aber das Muster
gefällt mir nicht.

(Pause.)

W. Umsteigen !

A. Welchen Hund haben Sie ? Haben Sie

den hübschen Hund des Kaufmanns, oder den hässlichen Hund der Urgrossmutter des Lehrlings des bogenbeinigen Zimmermanns?

W. (*Aside.*) Oh, come, she's ringing in a cold deck on us: that's Ollendorff.

GEO. Ich habe nicht den Hund des—des —(*Aside.*) Stuck! That's no Meisterschaft; they don't play fair. (*Aloud.*) Ich habe nicht den Hund des — des— In unserem Buche leider, gibt es keinen Hund; daher, ob ich auch gern von solchen Thieren sprechen möchte, ist es mir doch unmöglich, weil ich nicht vorbereitet bin. Entschuldigen Sie, meine Damen.

GR (*Aside.*) Beim Teufel, sie sind *alle* blödsinnig geworden. In meinem Leben habe ich nie ein so närrisches, verfluchtes, verdammtes Gespräch gehört

W. Bitte, umsteigen.

(Run the following rapidly through.)

M. (*Aside.*) Oh, I've flushed an easy batch! (*Aloud.*) Würden Sie mir erlauben meine Reisetasche hier hinzustellen?

GR. (*Aside.*) Wo ist seine Reisetasche?
Ich sehe keine.

W. Bitte sehr.

GEO. Ist meine Reisetasche Ihnen im
Wege?

GR. (*Aside.*) Und wo ist *seine* Reisetasche?

A. Erlauben Sie mir Sie von meiner Reisetasche zu befreien.

GR. (*Aside.*) Du Esel!

W. Ganz und gar nicht. (*To Geo.*) Es ist
sehr schwül in diesem Coupé.

GR. (*Aside.*) Coupè.

GEO. Sie haben Recht. Erlauben Sie mir,
gefälligst, das Fenster zu öffnen. Ein wenig
Luft würde uns got thun.

M. Wir fahren sehr rasch.

A. Haben Sie den Namen jener Station
gehört?

W. Wie lange halten wir auf dieser Station
an?

GEO. Ich reise nach Dresden, Schaffner.
Wo muss ich umsteigen?

A. Sie steigen nicht um, Sie bleiben sitzen.

GR. (*Aside.*) Sie sind ja alle ganz und gar

verrückt! Man denke sich sie glauben dass
sie auf der Eisenbahn reisen.

GEO. (*Aside, to William*) Now brace up;
pull all your confidence together, my boy, and
we'll try that lovely good-bye business a
flutter. I think it's about the gaudiest thing in
the book, if you boom it right along and don't
get left on a base. It'll impress the girls.
(*Aloud.*) Lassen Sie uns gehen: es ist schon
sehr spät, und ich muss morgen ganz früh
aufstehen.

GR. (*Aside—grateful.*) Gott sei Dank dass
sie endlich gehen. (*Sets her gun aside.*)

W. (*To Geo.*) Ich danke Ihnen höflichst für
die Ehre die sie mir erweisen, aber ich kann
nicht länger bleiben.

GEO. (*To W.*) Entschuldigen Sie mich gü-
tigst, aber ich kann wirklich nicht länger
bleiben.

Gretchen looks on stupefied.

W. (*To Geo.*) Ich habe schon eine Ein-
ladung angenommen; ich kann wirklich nicht
länger bleiben.

Gretchen fingers her gun again.

GEO. (*To W.*) Ich muss gehen.

W. (*To Geo.*) Wie! Sie wollen schon wieder gehen? Sie sind ja eben erst gekommen.

M. (*Aside*). It's just music!

A. (*Aside.*) Oh, how lovely they do it!

GEO. (*To W.*) Also denken sie doch noch nicht an's Gehen.

W. (*To Geo.*) Es thut mir unendlich leid, aber ich muss nach Hause. Meine Frau wird sich wundern, was aus mir geworden ist.

GEO. (*To W.*) Meine Frau hat keine Ahnung wo ich bin: ich muss wirklich jetzt fort.

W. (*To Geo.*) Dann will ich Sie nicht länger aufhalten; ich bedaure sehr dass Sie uns einen so kurzen Besuch gemacht haben.

GEO. (*To W.*) Adieu—auf recht baldiges Wiedersehen.

W. UMSTEIGEN!

Great hand-clapping from the girls.

M. (*Aside.*) Oh, how perfect! how elegant!

A. (*Aside.*) Per-fectly enchanting!

JOYOUS CHORUS. (*All.*) Ich habe gehabt,

du hast gehabt, er hat gehabt, wir haben gehabt, ihr habet gehabt, sie haben gehabt.

Gretchen faints, and tumbles from her chair, and the gun goes off with a crash. Each girl, frightened, seizes the protecting hand of her sweetheart. Gretchen scrambles up. Tableau.

W. (*Takes out some money—beckons Gretchen to him. George adds money to the pile.*) Hübsches Mädchen (*giving her some of the coins*), hast Du etwas gesehen?

GR. (*Courtesy—aside.*) Der Engel! (*Aloud —impressively.*) Ich habe nichts gesehen.

W. (*More money.*) Hast Du etwas gehört?

GR. Ich habe nichts gehört.

W. (*More money.*) Und Morgen?

GR. Morgen—wäre es nöthig—bin ich taub und blind.

W. Unvergleichbares Mädchen! Und (*giving the rest of the money*) darnach?

GR. (*Deep courtesy—aside.*) Erzengel! (*Aloud.*) Darnach, mien gnädgister, betrachten Sie mich also *taub—blind—todt!*

ALL. (*In chorus—with reverent joy.*) Ich habe gehabt, du hast gehabt, er hat gehabt, wir haben gehabt, ihr habet gehabt, sie haben gehabt!

ACT III.

Three weeks later.

SCENE I.

Enter Gretchen, and puts her shawl on a chair. Brushing around with the traditional feather-duster of the drama. Smartly dressed, for she is prosperous.

GR. Wie hätte man sich das vorstellen können! In nur drei Wochen bin ich schon reich geworden! (*Gets out of her pocket handful after handful of silver, which she piles on the table, and proceeds to re-pile and count, occasionally ringing or biting a piece to try its quality.*) Oh, dass (*with a sigh*) die Frau Wirthin nur *ewig* krank bliebe! . . . . Diese edlen jungen Männer—sie sind ja so liebenswürdig! Und so fleissig!—und so treu! Jeden Morgen kommen sie gerade um drei Viertel auf neun; und plaudern und schwatzen, und plappern, und schnattern, die jungen Damen auch; um Schlage zwölf nehmen sie Abschied; um Schlage eins kommen sie schon

wieder, und plaudern und schwatzen und
plappern und schnattern; gerade um sechs
Uhr nehmen sie wiederum Abschied; um halb
acht kehren sie noch'emal zurück, und plaudern und schwatzen und plappern und schnattern bis zehn Uhr, oder vielleicht ein Viertel
nach, falls ihre Uhren nach gehen (und stets
gehen sie nach am Ende des Besuchs, aber
stets vor Beginn desselben), und zuweilen un-
terhalten sich die jungen Leute beim Spaz-
ierengehen; und jeden Sonntag gehen sie
dreimal in die Kirche; und immer plaudern
sie, und schwatzen und plappern und schnattern bis ihnen die Zähnen aus dem Munde
fallen. Und *ich?* Durch Mangel an Uebung,
ist mir die Zunge mit Moos belegt worden!
Freilich ist's mir eine dumme Zeit gewesen.
Aber—um Gotteswillen, was geht das mir an?
Was soll ich daraus machen? Täglich sagt
die Frau Wirthin "Gretchen" (*dumb-show of
paying a piece of money into her hand*), "du
bist eine der besten Sprach-Lehrerinnen der
Welt!" Ach, Gott! Und täglich sagen die
edlen jungen Männer, "Gretchen, liebes

Kind" (*money-paying again in dumb-show—three coins*), "bleib' taub—blind—todt!" und so bleibe ich. . . . . Jetzt wird es ungefähr neun Uhr sein; bald kommen sie vom Spaziergehen zurück. Also, es wäre gut dass ich meinem eigenen Schatz einen Besuch abstatte und spazieren gehe. (*Dons her shawl.*)

Exit. L.

Enter Wirthin. R.

WIRTHIN. That was Mr. Stephenson's train that just came in. Evidently the girls are out walking with Gretchen;—can't find *them*, and *she* doesn't seem to be around. (*A ring at the door.*) That's him. I'll go see.

Exit. R.

Enter Stephenson and Wirthin. R.

S. Well, how does sickness seem to agree with you?

WIRTHIN. So well that I've never been out of my room since, till I heard your train come in.

S. Thou miracle of fidelity! Now I argue from that, that the new plan is working.

WIRTHIN. Working? Mr. Stephenson, you never saw anything like it in the whole course of your life! It's absolutely wonderful the way it works.

S. Succeeds? No—you don't mean it.

WIRTHIN. Indeed I do mean it. I tell you, Mr. Stephenson, that plan was just an inspiration—that's what it was. You could teach a cat German by it.

S. Dear me, this is noble news! Tell me about it.

WIRTHIN. Well, it's all Gretchen — ev-ery bit of it. I told you she was a jewel. And then the sagacity of that child—why, I never dreamed it was in her. Sh-she, "Never you ask the young ladies a question—never let on —just keep mum—leave the whole thing to me," sh-she.

S. Good! And she justified, did she?

WIRTHIN. Well, sir, the amount of German gabble that that child crammed into those two girls inside the next forty-eight hours—well, *I* was satisfied! So I've never asked a question —never *wanted* to ask any. I've just lain

curled up there, happy. The little dears ! they
've flitted in to see me a moment, every morning and noon and supper-time ; and as sure as
I'm sitting here, inside of six days they were
clattering German to me like a house afire !

S. Sp-lendid, splendid !

WIRTHIN. Of course it ain't grammatical—
the inventor of the language can't talk grammatical ; if the Dative didn't fetch him the Accusative would ; but it's German all the same,
and don't you forget it !

S. Go on—go on—this is delicious news—

WIRTHIN. Gretchen, she says to me at the
start, " Never you mind about company for
'em," sh-she—" I'm company enough." And
I says, " All right — fix it your own way,
child "; and that she *was* right is shown by the
fact that to this day they don't care a straw for
any company but hers.

S. Dear me ; why, it's admirable !

WIRTHIN. Well, I should think so! They just
dote on that hussy—can't seem to get enough
of her. Gretchen tells me so herself. And the
care she takes of them ! She tells me that

every time there's a moonlight night she coaxes them out for a walk ; and if a body can believe her, she actually bullies them off to church three times every Sunday !

S. Why, the little dev—missionary ! Really, she's a genius !

WIRTHIN. She's a bud, *I* tell you ! Dear me, how she's brought those girls' health up ! Cheeks ?—just roses. Gait ? — they walk on watch-springs ! And happy ?—by the bliss in their eyes, you 'd think they're in Paradise ! Ah, that Gretchen ! Just you imagine *our* trying to achieve these marvels !

S. You're right—every time. Those girls— why, all they 'd have wanted to know was what we wanted done—and then they wouldn't have *done* it—the mischievous young rascals !

WIRTHIN. Don't tell *me ?* Bless you, I found that out early—when *I* was bossing.

S. Well, I'm im - mensely pleased. *Now* fetch them down. I'm not afraid now. They won't want to go home.

WIRTHIN. Home ! I don't believe you could drag them away from Gretchen with nine span of horses. But if you want to see them, put on your hat and come along; they're out somewhere trapsing along with Gretchen. (*Going.*)

S. I'm with you—lead on.

WIRTHIN. We'll go out the side door. It's toward the Anlage.

Exit both. L.

Enter George and Margaret. R.

Her head lies upon his shoulder, his arm is about her waist; they are steeped in sentiment.

M. (*Turning a fond face up at him.*) Du Engel!

G. Liebste! (*Kiss.*)

M. Oh, das Liedchen dass Du mir gewidmet hast—es ist so schön, so wunderschön. Wie hätte ich je geahnt dass Du ein Poët wärest!

G. Mein Schätzchen!—es ist mir lieb wenn Dir die Kleinigkeit gefällt.

M. Ah, es ist mit der zärtlichsten Musik gefüllt—klingt ja so süss und selig—wie das Flüstern des Sommerwindes die Abenddämmerung hindurch. Wieder,—Theuerste!—sag' es wieder.

G.   Du bist wie eine Blume!—
          So schön und hold und rein—
       Ich schau Dich an, und Wehmuth
          Schleicht mir ins Herz hinein.
       Mir ist als ob ich die Hände
          Aufs Haupt Dir legen sollt,
       Betend dass Gott Dich erhalte,
          So rein und schön und hold.

M. A-ch! (*Dumb-show sentimentalisms.*)
Georgie—

   G. Kindchen!

   M. Warum kommen sie nicht?

   G. Dass weiss ich gar nicht. Sie waren—

   M. Es wird spät. Wir müssen sie antreiben.
Komm!

   G. Ich glaube sie werden recht bald ankommen, aber—

                    Exit both. L.

Enter Gretchen, R., in a state of mind. Slumps into
a chair limp with despair.

GR. Ach! was wird jetzt aus mir werden!
Zufällig habe ich in der Ferne den verdamm-
ten Papa gesehen!—und die Frau Wirthin
auch! Oh, diese Erscheinung,—die hat mir
beinahe das Leben genommen. Sie suchen
die jungen Damen—das weiss ich wenn sie

diese und die jungen Herren zusammen fänden
—du heiliger Gott! Wenn das geschicht,
wären wir Alle ganz und gar verloren! Ich
muss sie gleich finden, und ihr eine Warnung
geben!

Exit. L.

Enter Annie and Will. R.

Posed like the former couple and sentimental.

A. Ich liebe sich schon so sehr—Deiner edlen Natur wegen. Dass du dazu auch ein Dich-
ter bist!—ach, mein Leben ist uebermässig
reich geworden! Wir hätte sich doch einbilden
können dass ich einen Mann zu einem so wun-
derschönen Gedicht hätte begeistern können!

W. Liebste! Es ist nur eine Kleinigkeit.

A. Nein, nein, es ist ein echtes Wunder!
Sage es noch einmal—ich flehe Dich an.

W.   Du bist wie eine Blume!—
         So schön und hold und rein—
     Ich schau Dich an, und Wehmuth
         Schleicht mir ins Herz hinein.
     Mir ist als ob ich die Hände
         Aufs Haupt Dir legen sollt,
     Betend dass Gott Dich erhalte,
         So rein und schön und hold.

A. Ach, es ist himmlisch—einfach himmlisch. (*Kiss.*) Schreibt auch George Gedichte?

W. Oh, ja—zuweilen.

A. Wie schön!

W. (*Aside.*) Smouches 'em, same as I do! It was a noble good idea to play that little thing on her. George wouldn't ever think of that—somehow he never had any invention.

A. (*Arranging chairs.*) Jetzt will ich bei Dir sitzen bleiben, und Du—

W. (*They sit.*) Ja,—und ich—

A. Du wirst mir die alte Geschichte die immer neu bleibt, noch wieder erzählen.

W. Zum Beispiel, dass ich Dich liebe!

A. Wieder!

W. Ich—sie kommen!

　　　Enter George and Margaret.

A. Das macht nichts. Fortan!

(*George unties M.'s bonnet. She re-ties his cravat—interspersings of love-pats, etc., and dumb-show of love-quarrelings.*)

W. Ich liebe Dich.

A. Ach! Noch einmal!

W. Ich habe Dich von Herzen lieb.

A. Ach! Abermals!

W. Bist Du denn noch nicht satt?

A. Nein! (*The other couple sit down, and Margaret begins a re-tying of the cravat. Enter the Wirthin and Stephenson, he imposing silence with a sign.*) Mich hungert sehr, ich verhungre!

W. Oh, Du armes Kind! (*Lays her head on his shoulder. Dumb-show between Stephenson and Wirthin.*) Und hungert es nicht mich? Du hast mir nicht einmal gesagt—

A. Dass ich Dich liebe? Mein Eigener! (*Frau Wirthin threatens to faint—is supported by Stephenson.*) Höre mich nur an: Ich liebe Dich, ich liebe Dich—

Enter Gretchen.

GR. (*Tears her hair.*) Oh, dass ich in der Hölle wäre!

M. Ich liebe Dich, ich liebe Dich! Ah, ich bin so glücklich dass ich nicht schlafen kann, nicht lesen kann, nicht reden kann, nicht—

A. Und ich! Ich bin auch so glücklich dass ich nicht speisen kann, nicht studieren, arbeiten, denken, schreiben—

STEPHENSON. (*To . Wirthin — aside.*) Oh, there isn't any mistake about it—Gretchen's just a rattling teacher!

WIRTHIN. (*To Stephenson—aside.*) I'll skin her alive when I get my hands on her!

M. Komm, alle Verliebte! (*They jump up, join hands, and sing in chorus*)—

> Du, Du, wie ich Dich liebe,
> Du, Du, liebst auch mich!
> Die, die zärtlichsten Triebe—

S. (*Stepping forward.*)   Well!

The girls throw themselves upon his neck with enthusiasm.

THE GIRLS. Why, father!

S. My darlings!

The young men hesitate a moment, then they add their embrace, flinging themselves on Stephenson's neck, along with the girls.

THE YOUNG MEN. Why, father!

S. (*Struggling.*) Oh come, this is too thin! —too quick, I mean.   Let go, you rascals!

GEO. We'll never let go till you put us on the family list.

M. Right! hold to him!

A. Cling to him, Will!

Gretchen rushes in and joins the general embrace, but is snatched away by the Wirthin, crushed up against the wall and threatened with destruction.

S. (*Suffocating.*) All right, all right—have it your own way, you quartette of swindlers!

W. He's a darling! Three cheers for papa!

EVERYBODY. (*Except Stephenson who bows with hand on heart.*) Hip—hip—hip: hurrah, hurrah, hurrah!

GR. Der Tiger—ah-h-h!

WIRTHIN. Sei ruhig, you hussy!

S. Well, I've lost a couple of precious daughters, but I've gained a couple of precious scamps to fill up the gap with ; so it's all right. I'm satisfied, and everybody's forgiven—(*With mock threats at Gretchen.*)

W. Oh, wir werden für Dich sorgen — du herrliches Gretchen!

GR. Danke schön !

M. (*To Wirthin.*) Und für Sie auch ; denn wenn Sie nicht so freundlich gewesen wären, krank zu werden, wie wären wir je so glücklich geworden wie jetzt ?

WIRTHIN. Well, dear, I *was* kind, but I didn't mean it.   But I ain't sorry—not one bit —that I ain't.

Tableau.

S. Come now, the situation is full of hope, and grace, and tender sentiment.   If I had in the least the poetic gift, I know I could impro-vise under such an inspiration (*each girl nudges her sweetheart*) something worthy to—to—is there no poet among us ?

Each youth turns solemnly his back upon the other and raises his hands in benediction over his sweet-heart's bowed head.
Both youths at once.

Mir ist als ob ich die Hände
Aus Haupt Dir legen sollt—

They turn and look reproachfully at each other—the girls contemplate them with injured surprise.

S. (*Reflectively.*) I think I've heard that before somewhere.

WIRTHIN. (*Aside.*) Why the very cats in
Germany know it!

Curtain.

CHARLES L. WEBSTER & CO.

William Sharp.

Flower o' the Vine: Romantic Ballads and Sospiri di Roma.—This volume contains the poems in Mr. Sharp's latest books of verse, now entirely out of print. His collaboration with Blanche Willis Howard in the novel " A Fellowe and His Wife," has made his name familiar to American readers. As one of the most popular of the younger English poets, we anticipate an equal success in America for " Flower o' the Vine," for which Mr. Thomas A. Janvier has prepared an Introduction. Handsomely bound, uniform with Aldrich's " Sisters' Tragedy " and Cora Fabbri's " Lyrics." Cloth, $1.50.

Dan Beard.

Moonblight and Three Feet of Romance.—Octavo, 300 pages, fully illustrated. This story we believe will take rank with " Looking Backward." It treats of some of the great social problems of the day in a novel, powerful, and intensely interesting manner. The hero becomes strangely endowed with the power of seeing people in their true light. It is needless to say that this power proves both a curse and a blessing, and leads to many and strange adventures. Mr. Beard's reputation as an artist is world-wide, and the numerous illustrations he provides for this book powerfully portray the spirit of the text. Cloth, ink and gold stamps, $2.00.

Mark Twain's Books.

Adventures of Huckleberry Finn.—Holiday edition. Square 8vo, 366 pages. Illustrated by E. W. Kemble. Sheep, $3.25; cloth, $2.75.

New Cheap Edition of Huckleberry Finn.—12mo, 318 pages, with a few illustrations. Cloth, $1.00.

The Prince and the Pauper.—A square 8vo volume of 411 pages. Beautifully illustrated. Sheep $3.75; cloth, $3.00.

A Connecticut Yankee in King Arthur's Court.— A square 8vo of 575 pages; 221 illustrations by Dan Beard. Half morocco, $5.00; sheep, $4.00; cloth, $3.00.

Mark Twain Holiday Set.—Three volumes in a box, consisting of the best editions of "Huckleberry Finn," "Prince and Pauper," and "A Connecticut Yankee." Square 8vo. Uniform in size, binding, and color. Sold only in sets. Cloth, $6.00.

Eighteen Short Stories and Sketches.—By Mark Twain. Including "The Stolen White Elephant," "Some Rambling Notes," "The Carnival of Crime," "A Curious Experience," "Punch, Brothers, Punch," "The Invalid's Story," etc., etc. 16mo, 306 pages. Cloth, $1.00.

Mark Twain's "Library of Humor."—A volume of 145 Characteristic Selections from the Best Writers, together with a Short Biographical Sketch of Each Author quoted. Compiled by Mark Twain. Nearly 200 illustrations by E. W Kemble. 8vo, 707 pages. Full Turkey morocco, $7.00; half morocco, $5.00; half seal, $4.25; sheep, $4.00; cloth, $3.50.

Life on the Mississippi.—8vo, 624 pages; and over 300 illustrations. Sheep, $4.25; cloth, $3.50.

Innocents Abroad; or, The New Pilgrim's Progress. Sheep, $4.00; cloth, $3.50.

Roughing It.—600 pages; 300 illustrations. Sheep, $4.00; cloth, $3.50.

Sketches, Old and New.—320 pages; 122 illustrations. Sheep, $3.50; cloth, $3.00.

Adventures of Tom Sawyer.—150 engravings; 275 pages. Sheep, $3.25; cloth, $2.75.

The Gilded Age.—576 pages; 212 illustrations. Sheep, $4.00; cloth, $3.50.

A Tramp Abroad. Mark Twain in Europe.—A Companion Volume to "Innocents Abroad." 631 pages. Sheep, $4.00; cloth, $3.50.

The War Series.

The Genesis of the Civil War.—The Story of Sumter, by Major-General S. W. Crawford, A. M., M. D., LL. D. Illustrated with steel and wood engravings and fac-similes of celebrated letters. 8vo, uniform with Grant's Memoirs. Full morocco, $8.00; half morocco, $5.50; sheep, $4.25; cloth, $3.50.

Personal Memoirs of General Grant.—Illustrations and maps, etc. 2 vols.; 8vo. Half morocco, per set, $11.00; sheep, per set, $6.00; cloth, per set, $7.00. A few sets in full Turkey morocco and tree calf for sale at special low prices.

Personal Memoirs of General Sherman.—With appendix by Hon. James G. Blaine. Illustrated; 2 vols.; 8vo, uniform with Grant's Memoirs. Half morocco, per set, $8.50; sheep, per set, $7.00; cloth, per set, $5.00. Cheap edition, in one large volume. Cloth, $2.00.

Personal Memoirs of General Sheridan.—Illustrated with steel portraits and woodcuts; 26 maps; 2 vols.; 8vo, uniform with Grant's Memoirs. Half morocco, per set, $10.00; sheep, per set, $8.00; cloth, per set, $6.00. A few sets in full Turkey morocco and tree calf to be disposed of at very low figures. Cheap edition, in one large volume, cloth binding, $2.00.

McClellan's Own Story.— With illustrations from sketches drawn on the field of battle by A. R. Waud, the Great War Artist. 8vo, uniform with Grant's Memoirs. Full morocco, $9.00; half morocco, $6.00; sheep, $4.75; cloth, $3.75.

Memoirs of John A. Dahlgren.— Rear-Admiral United States Navy. By his widow, Madeleine Vinton Dahlgren. A large octavo volume of 660 pages, with steel portrait, maps and illustrations. Cloth, $3.00.

Reminiscences of Winfield Scott Hancock.—By his wife. Illustrated; steel portraits of General and Mrs. Hancock; 8vo, uniform with Grant's Memoirs. Full morocco, $5.00; half morocco, $4.00; sheep, $3.50; cloth, $2.75.

Tenting on the Plains. — With the Life of General Custer, by Mrs. E. B. Custer. Illustrated; 8vo, uniform with Grant's Memoirs. Full morocco, $7.00; half morocco, $5.50; sheep, $4.25; cloth, $3.50.

Portrait of General Sherman.—A magnificent line etching on copper; size 19x24 inches; by the celebrated artist, Charles B. Hall. $2.00. (Special prices on quantities.)

The Great War Library.—Consisting of the best editions of the foregoing seven publications (Grant, Sheridan, Sherman, Hancock, McClellan, Custer and Crawford). Ten volumes in a box; uniform in style and binding. Half morocco, $50.00; sheep, $40.00; cloth, $30.00.

Other Biographical Works.

Life of Jane Welsh Carlyle. — By Mrs. Alexander Ireland. With portrait and fac-simile letter; 8vo, 324 pages. Vellum cloth, gilt top, $1.75.

Life and Letters of Roscoe Conkling. — By Hon. Alfred R. Conkling, Ph. B., LL.D.; steel portrait and fac-similes of important letters to Conkling from Grant, Arthur, Garfield, etc. 8vo, over 700 pages. Half morocco, $5.50; full seal, $5.00; sheep, $4.00; cloth, $3.00.

Life of Pope Leo XIII. — By Bernard O'Reilly, D. D., L. D. (Laval.) Written with the encouragement and blessing of His Holiness, the Pope. 8vo, 635 pages; colored and steel plates, and full-page illustrations. Half morocco, $6.00; half Russia, $5.00; cloth, gilt edges, $3.75.

Distinguished American Lawyers. — With their Struggles and Triumphs in the Forum. Containing an elegantly engraved portrait, autograph and biography of each subject, embracing the professional work and the public career of those called to serve their country. By Henry W. Scott. Introduction by Hon. John J. Ingalls. A large royal octavo volume of 716 pages, with 62 portraits of the most eminent lawyers. Sheep, $4.25; cloth, $3.50.

Miscellaneous.

Concise Cyclopedia of Religious Knowledge.— Biblical, Biographical, Theological, Historical and Practical; edited by Rev. E. B. Sanford, M. A., assisted by over 30 of the most eminent religious scholars in the country. 1 vol.; royal 8vo, nearly 1,000 double-column pages. Half morocco, $6.00; sheep, $5.00; cloth, $3.50.

The Table.—How to Buy Food, How to Cook It, and How to Serve It, by A. Filippini, of Delmonico's; the only cook-book ever endorsed by Delmonico; contains three menus for each day in the year, and over 1,500 original recipes, the most of which have been guarded as secrets by the *chefs* of Delmonico. Contains the simplest as well as the most elaborate recipes. Presentation edition in full seal Russia, $4.50; Kitchen edition in oil-cloth, $2.50.

One Hundred Ways of Cooking Eggs.—Mr. Filippini is probably the only man who can cook eggs in a hundred different ways, and this little book will be worth its price ten times over to any purchaser. Cloth binding, ink and gold stamps, 50 cents.

Also uniform with the above,

One Hundred Recipes for Cooking and Serving Fish.—This book contains only the best recipes, all of which have been tested by Mr. Filippini during 25 years' experience with the Delmonicos. Cloth binding, ink and gold stamps, 50 cents.

Yale Lectures on Preaching, and other Writings, by Rev. Nathaniel Burton, D. D.; edited by Richard E. Burton. 8vo, 640 pages; steel portrait. Cloth, $3.75.

Legends and Myths of Hawaii.—By the late King Kalakaua; two steel portraits and 25 other illustrations. 8vo, 530 pages. Cloth, $3.00.

The Diversions of a Diplomat in Turkey.—By the late Hon. S. S. Cox. 8vo, 685 pages; profusely illustrated. Half morocco, $6.00; sheep, $4.75; cloth, $3.75.

Inside the White House in War Times.—By W. O. Stoddard, one of Lincoln's Private Secretaries. 12mo, 244 pages. Cloth, $1.00.

Tinkletop's Crime, and eighteen other Short Stories, by George R. Sims. 1 vol.; 12mo, 316 pages. Cloth, $1.00; paper covers, 50 cents.

My Life with Stanley's Rear Guard.—By Herbert Ward, one of the Captains of Stanley's Rear Guard; includes Mr. Ward's Reply to H. M. Stanley. 12mo. Cloth, $1.00; paper covers, 50 cents.

The Peril of Oliver Sargent.—By Edgar Janes Bliss. 12mo. Cloth, $1.00; paper covers, 50 cents.

The Old Devil and the Three Little Devils; or, Ivan The Fool, by Count Leo Tolstoi, translated direct from the Russian by Count Norraikow, with illustrations by the celebrated Russian artist, Gribayédoff. 12mo. Cloth, $1.00.

Life IS Worth Living, and Other Stories.— Translated direct from the Russian by Count Norraikow. This work, unlike some of his later writings, shows the great Russian at his best. The stories are pure, simple and powerful; intensely interesting as mere creations of fancy, but, like all Tolstoi's works, written for a purpose, and containing abundant food for earnest reflection. Cloth, ink and gold stamps, $1.00.

The Happy Isles, and Other Poems, by S. H. M. Byers. Small 12mo. Cloth binding, $1.00.

Physical Beauty; How to Obtain and How to Preserve It, by Annie Jenness Miller; including chapters on Hygiene, Foods, Sleep, Bodily Expression, the Skin, the Eyes, the Teeth, the Hair, Dress, the Cultivation of Individuality, etc., etc. An octavo volume of about 300 pages. Cloth, $2.00.

Hour-Glass Series.—By Daniel B. Lucas, LL. D., and J. Fairfax McLaughlin, LL. D. The first volume, which is now ready, contains a series of historical epitomes of national interest, with interesting sketches of such men as Henry Clay, Daniel O'Connell and Fisher Ames. Large 12mo. Cloth, $1.00.

Adventures of A Fair Rebel.—Author of "'Zeki'l," "Bet Crow," "S'phiry Ann," "Was It an Exceptional Case?" etc. A story that is sure to be eagerly sought after and read by Miss Crim's many admirers. Stamped cloth, $1.00; paper covers, 50 cents.

In Beaver Cove and Elsewhere.—Octavo, about 350
pages, illustrated.

PRESS OPINIONS.

" A writer who has quickly won wide recognition by short
stories of exceptional power."—*New York Independent.*
" Her magazine articles bear the stamp of genius."—*St. Paul
Globe.*
This volume contains all of Miss Crim's most famous
short stories. These stories have received the highest
praise from eminent critics and prominent literary journals, and have given Miss Crim a position among the
leading lady writers of America. Cloth, handsomely
stamped, $1.00; paper covers, 50 cents.

The Flowing Bowl: What and When to Drink ; by
the only William (William Schmidt); giving full instructions how to prepare, mix, and serve drinks: also
receipts for 227 Mixed Drinks, 89 Liquors and Ratafias,
115 Punches, 58 Bowls, and 29 Extra Drinks. An 8vo
of 300 pages. Fine cloth, gilt stamp, $2.00.

AFTERWORD

Forrest G. Robinson

There is little reason to believe that Mark Twain gave much thought to the planning and publication of *Merry Tales*. When the volume appeared in April 1892, its author was living with his family in Europe. They had gone abroad the year before, in part as a measure of economy, and in part on the hope that the change might be good for Mark Twain's wife, Livy, who suffered from heart troubles. The Clemens children — Susy, Clara, and Jean — attended boarding schools in Switzerland and Germany, while their parents settled in Berlin, then traveled south during the spring months to France and Italy in search of good health. The sojourn in Europe was in fact to become a permanent way of life for America's leading humorist and his family, who remained abroad for most of the next decade.

Eighteen ninety-two was a hard year in a hard period of Mark Twain's life. His beloved mother succumbed to a stroke in late 1890; Livy's mother died just a month later. Equally upsetting, his youngest daughter, Jean, had begun to betray the symptoms of what would later be diagnosed as epilepsy. Nor was Twain's health much stronger than Livy's. He battled rheumatism, pneumonia, and assorted minor afflictions which served as painful reminders of his advancing years (he would be fifty in 1895). His writing fared no better. *A Connecticut Yankee in King Arthur's Court* (1889) sold only moderately well, and prompted him to look for ways to retire from the literary profession. But there would be no relief for the weary writer, who found in his pen the sole and finally insufficient bulwark against collapsing finances. While he would in time produce such important works as *Pudd'nhead Wilson* (1894) and

Following the Equator (1897), the Lincoln of our literature had entered a period of gradual creative decline from which he would never fully recover.

Money and writing were fatefully intertwined in the life of Mark Twain. His fortunes peaked in 1885 with the appearance of *Huckleberry Finn* and the completion of the *Personal Memoirs of U. S. Grant*, a publishing venture that yielded substantial dividends both to its deceased author's family and to Twain's recently founded publishing firm, Charles L. Webster and Company. But the elements of a major downfall were also beginning to surface. Most crucially, he was investing more and more heavily in a typesetting machine invented by James W. Paige. This mechanical marvel, which seemed to promise a bonanza in profits but in fact never worked, was a heavy drain on resources for more than a decade. When bankruptcy finally came in 1894, Twain wisely delivered the management of his business affairs into the capable hands of his new friend Henry Huttleston Rogers, the Standard Oil mogul. Thanks to Rogers' sage counsel, and to the profits from a round-the-world lecture tour, the shattered humorist was eventually restored to financial security and a modicum of self-respect. But the failed dream of vast personal wealth formed the dark prologue to a series of painful setbacks — most especially the deaths of Susy, Livy, and Jean — which punctuated the last years of Twain's life. He died in 1910.

The publication of *Merry Tales* may be viewed as a minor episode in the much larger drama of Mark Twain's financial collapse. By 1892, as Paige's temperamental machine drew him ever deeper into debt, Twain looked to his publishing company, which was also failing, for a timely boost. On the initiative of his partner, Fred Hall, who took charge of the business when Twain fled to Europe in 1891, Webster and Company issued the Fiction, Fact, and Fancy series of trade books (seventy-five cents in cloth bindings, twenty-five cents in paper) designed to sell quickly and in large quantities to a popular audience hungry for inexpensive entertainment. Hence *Merry Tales*, which numbered among the volumes in the series, is described in the opening "Editor's Note" as ranking with "the better class of native literature" now available "at moderate prices." But even at bargain rates the collection sold poorly, and thus contributed in a small way to the eventual undoing of its author.

Mark Twain may have taken some part in selecting the stories to be included in *Merry Tales*; otherwise, there is no evidence of his personal involvement in the book's production and marketing. Perhaps he was indifferent to the venture; more likely, he was too far from home, and too much taken up with other, more pressing matters, to concern himself closely with its publication. We do know that in later years he took a dim view of the volume. When Harper and Brothers commenced planning for an 1897 reissue of *Merry Tales*, Mark Twain pleaded, "[P]lease squelch that title & call the mess by some other name — almost *any* other name. Webster and Company invented that silly title."[†] It requires no great stretch of the critical imagination to understand this grumbling at the book's "silly title." Granted, there is humor enough scattered through the stories; but little of it qualifies as "merry." More to the point, perhaps, the unhappy author clearly implies that the selections in the book sit rather awkwardly together, and possess in the aggregate little unity or coherence. As a collection, in short, they are a "mess."

The early critics of *Merry Tales* seem to have reached a similarly negative assessment — or such we may surmise from the resounding silence that greeted the book's publication. The very slender response may have registered an awareness that most of the items in the volume had been published before; perhaps, too, the critics were inclined to veer away from marketing schemes such as the Fiction, Fact, and Fancy series. In any case, only two brief notices have turned up to mark the appearance of *Merry Tales*. The *New York Independent* issued a few words of praise ("This volume shows Mr. Clemens at his very best"), while the *Mahogany Tree*, a Boston journal, more nearly approached Twain's own estimate. "Mr. Clemens," the anonymous reviewer declared, "is capable of better things than we have of late been receiving from his hand." If it is true that unfavorable reviews are better than no reviews at all, then *Merry Tales* fared very poorly. It should be added that subsequent generations of readers have registered little dissent from the virtual consensus of

[†] Mark Twain's previously unpublished words are © 1996 by Chemical Bank as Trustee of the Mark Twain Foundation, which reserves all reproduction or dramatization rights in every medium. Quotation is made with the permission of the University of California Press and Robert H. Hirst, General Editor, Mark Twain Project.

silence. Is there a book title in the Mark Twain oeuvre less readily recognized than this one?

But if the collection has languished in obscurity, its opening sketch, "The Private History of a Campaign That Failed," has not. In the century and more that has passed since the publication of *Merry Tales*, this striking autobiographical narrative has attracted far more attention than all the other stories in the volume combined. Indeed, "The Private History" is much more widely esteemed than the book in which it first appeared, and from which it is virtually always excerpted. It was perhaps in recognition of the importance of the story that the editors placed it first among the seven items in the collection. For present purposes, however, we will reverse that order, reserving the premier literary artifact for fuller discussion once the other tales have been dealt with.

"The Private History" is immediately followed by "The Invalid's Story," a rough and rather fragrant specimen of frontier humor, and a reminder that Victorian gentility often gave way to the grosser rudiments of life in Mark Twain's background and sensibility. (We may recall that his mother, though fragile and pious in her way, took enormous pleasure from her son's detailed descriptions of the fires that consumed lives and large buildings in the cities he visited. Life in Hannibal seems to have fostered an appetite for "realism" and "strong" subjects.) While "The Invalid's Story" afforded the humorist a very good laugh from a very bad smell, his friend William Dean Howells was not similarly moved by the jest. Originally designed as an installment in "Some Rambling Notes of an Idle Excursion," a series that Twain wrote for the *Atlantic Monthly* in 1877, the sketch struck Howells, the editor of the prestigious journal, as a little too pungent for his more fastidious subscribers, and he declined to publish it. Thus rejected, the story was pigeonholed for a few years, made its first appearance in *The Stolen White Elephant* (1882), and was duly returned to service a decade later in *Merry Tales*.

"The Invalid's Story" has attracted scant critical attention, though one discerning commentator has characterized the brief narrative as a parody of the themes and techniques to be found in the stories of Edgar Allan Poe. Certainly the narrator's opening complaint that horror has ruined his health — a sentiment echoed in the equally morbid, and ludicrous, conclusion to the tale — lends credence to this view. So does Twain's humorous management of suspense, and the tone of mock ghoulishness that pervades the piece. Still, the story's humorous authority is grounded most firmly in the figure of the old expressman, Thompson, whose brisk vernacular ("Pfew! I reckon it ain't no cinnamon 't I've loaded up thish-yer stove with!") and garbled references to Scripture are the sturdy staples of frontier literary art. His salty pronouncements sustain us, even as we navigate the awkward parenthetical contrivances with which the narrative is patched together. Like so much of Mark Twain's writing, the sketch succeeds in spite of its formal derelictions.

"The Captain's Story," another rerun, first saw the light of day as an installment in the aforementioned "Idle Excursion" series of 1877. The sketch features a variation on Twain's enduring preoccupation with innocence, here rather improbably on display in Captain "Hurricane" Jones, "a gray and bearded child" whom the narrator admires precisely because he is "simply an innocent, lovable old infant." The plentiful humor of the piece has its source in the hero's robust vernacular, and in the errant profundities of his biblical erudition. But even when he is inadvertently the butt of his equally inadvertent jokes, the captain is borne aloft on the wind of his own transcendent bluster. Based on Ned Wakeman, the flamboyant maritime folk hero of Mark Twain's California days, Hurricane Jones is an avatar of Captain Stormfield, the vernacular demigod and brash celestial pilot who for many years filled a large place in the humorist's imagination. In a rather different frame of reference, Jones' crackbrained interpretation of Isaac and the prophets of Baal is reminiscent, in its outrageous brand of trickery, to the stunts performed by Hank Morgan in the Camelot of *A Connecticut Yankee.*

The brief but positive review of *Merry Tales* in the *New York Independent* reserves special praise for "Mrs. McWilliams and the Lightning," which is on its own judged well "worth the price of the book." First published in the September 1880 number of the *Atlantic Monthly,* the story records an absurdly comical discussion between a henpecked husband and his phobic wife, who has been brought to the verge of panic by a late-night electrical storm. The humor of the piece turns on the couple's frantic attempt to agree on a rational explanation for the wife's irrational fears. We are reminded here of Tom Sawyer's fretful Aunt Polly, and of the panoply of superstition and pseudoscience with which frontier villagers armed themselves against the unknown. When it is finally discovered that the thunder and lightning are in fact the boom and flash of cannon firing from a nearby hill to celebrate the presidential nomination of James A. Garfield, we are afforded an oblique glimpse into the humorist's politics. The cannon bursts register his support for Garfield, the Republican dark horse and subsequent victor in the presidential election of 1880. To Twain's great disappointment, the celebration ended quite abruptly a year later, when Garfield fell to an assassin's bullet.

"Meisterschaft" stands out among the "merry tales" both because it is a play in three acts and because much of it is in German. The title of the little comedy, which may be translated "Champion-Maker," alludes to the Meisterschaft System, "A Short and Practical Method of Acquiring Complete Fluency of Speech in the German Language," developed by Dr. Richard S. Rosenthal, and published in Boston. For a mere five dollars, the aspiring linguist received a series of fifteen pamphlets containing three lessons each, plus "the privilege of asking, by letter, questions concerning each lesson." Similar courses were available on the same terms in French, Italian, and Spanish. Albert Bigelow Paine, Twain's first and "official" biographer, reported that his subject used the Meisterschaft System to study German in the late 1880s, and wrote the play to amuse friends who regularly joined him at his home to speak the language. The piece first appeared in the *Century* magazine of January 1888.

"Meisterschaft" is tribute to Mark Twain's success at mastering what he described — in a celebrated appendix to *A Tramp Abroad* (1880) — as "The Awful German Language." "A person who has not studied German," he there observes, "can form no idea of what a perplexing language it is." "Meisterschaft" is a humorous elaboration on that observation, but with the genial proviso that love triumphs over all obstacles, even the seemingly insurmountable barrier of a foreign language. Obliged as they are to conduct their courtship in German, the young lovers have — as the little drama amply demonstrates — a potent incentive to learning. They stumble along in laughably formal and old-fashioned constructions and scattered snatches of dialogue out of their textbooks; but of course the heart is equal to all challenges. Along the way, "Meisterschaft" demonstrates as well that Mark Twain was himself an accomplished student of the language he so loved to ridicule. Indeed, precisely because its humor is accessible only to those fluent in German, it seems unlikely that the audience for the play has ever been a very large one.

Two of the otherwise rather random selections in *Merry Tales* are related at least in their indirect bearing on the "The Private History of a Campaign That Failed." "Luck," first published in the August 1891 number of *Harper's New Monthly* magazine, is narrated by a familiar figure in Twain's work, a quondam "innocent" whose story records his emergence into "experience." The narrator learns, as his counterpart in *Roughing It* learns, that all that glitters is not gold. In this case, however, the overvaluation pertains not to pyrite but to human character — specifically, the character of a famous British military hero whose exploits in the Crimean War are not, as most people suppose, the products of his personal qualities but the results of blind luck. In reality, the celebrated hero is "an absolute fool" whom life has dealt an unbroken string of winning hands. To the accepted equation of success with virtue, then, the story responds with "proof that the very best thing in all this world that can befall a man is to be born lucky." Such undercutting of conventional pieties is of course a familiar humorous gambit with Mark Twain. But the subversion of putative military glory is a special instance, and brings to mind the similarly deflationary thrust of "The Private History of a Campaign That Failed." In both narratives we are witness to an impulse to diminish the heroic luster of military endeavors, at which Mark Twain, by his own admission in "The Private History," was an utter failure.

"A Curious Experience" commences in irrepressible energy and fun, but finds its way to a much darker corridor in Twain's imagination. Another of his deflationary renderings of military life, the piece appeared first in the *Century* magazine for November 1881 and was reissued the following year in *The Stolen White Elephant*. Curious indeed, it recounts at length and in considerable detail how a mere boy, his head full of dime novel adventures, contrives to persuade a Union officer that he is a Confederate spy. The youngster's delight in deception, we may suspect, reflects a similar sentiment on the part of Mark Twain, whose narrative, at once farfetched and plausible, has the "feel" of a hoax about it. Is the story's copious, realistic detail sufficient to win the full suspension of our disbelief? Are we persuaded that the narrative came to Mark Twain from the Union major mentioned at the outset? Skeptics may be interested to learn of a letter sent by "A Captious Reader" to the *Critic*, a respected New York literary weekly, in December 1881. The anonymous correspondent reported that he "soon recognized the story" set forth in "A Curious Experience" as "a true one, told me in the summer of 1878 by an officer of the U.S. Artillery. Query: Did Mr. Twain expect the public to credit this narrative to his clever brain?" The editors dutifully replied that the author had no wish to deceive his audience in any way, and educed as proof the "Note" about his "source," the major, that Mark Twain appended to the story. But of course in granting credibility to this exchange, we accept at face value the Captious Reader's declaration that the story is "a true one." Can we be sure that in assenting to this apparently casual claim we have not once again taken the bait?

We are on firmer ground in observing that "A Curious Experience" takes its place beside "Luck" as a story in which the solemnity and awe conventionally accorded military life are subtly undermined. The piece is set in "the winter of 1862–3," when Union forces were failing at Fredericksburg, and as Lincoln prepared to issue the Emancipation Proclamation. In place of real Civil War drama, however, Twain's narrative gives us a protracted false alarm set in motion by a child, but with sufficient skill and plausibility to bring the operations of a Union fort to complete confusion. It is all a harmless joke, after all. Nonetheless our response may be somewhat mixed. On one side, we are impressed and doubtless amused by the resourceful — if equally deceitful — boy, who in his pluck and imagination is the close literary kin of Tom Sawyer, Hank Morgan, and a host of mysterious strangers, young Satan among them. At the same time, the story may also form the occasion for much more solemn reflections on the vanity of war. Grown men, we are shown, can be stirred to suspicion, fear, anger, and violent action by a groundless fiction hatched in the overheated fantasies of a child. So construed, war is a tragedy arising from quixotic illusions and misapprehensions; it is part and parcel of the "disease" inflicted on the South, as Mark Twain argues in *Life on the Mississippi*, by the pernicious romances of Sir Walter Scott. Against this background, "The Private History of a Campaign That Failed" — in which the narrator reports that as a result of his brief wartime experience he "knew more about retreating than the man that invented retreating" — may appear as the record of a victory, albeit a somewhat inadvertent victory, over the palpable madness of war. Indeed, read in context with "A Curious Experience," this imperfect submergence of self-abasement in humor may seem, quite paradoxically, a species of transcendent sagacity.

"The Private History" is the best firsthand evidence we have on a pivotal episode in Mark Twain's life — his decision, after a few weeks of service in a Confederate unit, to abandon the war for the safer adventures that awaited him in faraway California and Nevada. It was obviously a difficult decision, and one whose interest is intensified for us by the fact that it produced permanent and potently mixed feelings in the mind of its maker. Part of Mark Twain yearned to take a hero's role in the great struggle that engulfed the nation in 1861. But another part of him — a stronger part, apparently — drew back from the conflict. Was his retreat the act of a coward? Mark Twain must have felt at times that facing that vexed question for the rest of his life was far worse than facing the Union army in 1861. The fear — at times the certainty — that others judged him a coward must have seemed a terrible penalty to pay for a perfectly human — arguably a perfectly rational — decision. At intervals he must have wished that he had it to do all over again; that given the opportunity, and knowing what he knew about the alternative, he would have faced death and seized his chance for glory. Most of all, we may reasonably surmise, he craved relief from the burden of guilt and anger and shame and injured pride — of vexed ambiguity — that the episode and its memory brought with them. In 1873, responding to his friend Charles Dudley Warner's request for a detailed summary of his life, Mark Twain made no reference to the experiences that he would later describe in "The Private History." It was as though he had gone directly from piloting on the Mississippi to prospecting in Nevada, without pausing briefly along the way to serve in a war.

As a title, "The Private History of a Campaign That Failed" refers both to the failure of Mark Twain's attempt to become a soldier, which is treated humorously, and to the killing of the anonymous stranger, which is set forth with considerable gravity. Such extremities of tone bespeak an ambivalence which is just as clearly evident when the title is taken to refer reflexively to the text itself. In this third reading, what fails is Mark Twain's attempt to construct a narrative coherent and believable and forgiving enough to permit emotional closure with the past. This uncertainty, the irreducible ambiguity at the heart of his approach to his material, may be said to constitute the sketch's moral significance. Traces of the same uncertainty surface in Twain's representation of himself as younger and much more naive — and therefore more readily forgiven — than he actually was in 1861. And if, as most scholars agree, the climactic killing is also a fiction, then there is a kindred variety of moral hedging at large in that episode's implied condemnation of war, and in its correlative justification for desertion. It is perfectly revealing in this regard that in a later rendering of "The Private History" the killing is treated as a species of dark comedy. Just so, Twain once toyed with the idea of making Huck and Tom and Jim the protagonists in a broadly humorous treatment of his wartime experiences. "I read your piece about the unsuccessful campaign," wrote William Dean Howells of the final, published version. "It was immensely amusing, with such a bloody bit of heartache in it, too."

There is an analogy of sorts to "The Private History" in a close call with conflict that overtook Mark Twain in 1864, while he was a reporter in Virginia City. It was a time of continued uncertainty for him, not least because his wartime loyalties were subject to constant shifts as the emergent, reconstructed Union man in him struggled with the diehard Southerner. The latter self — stimulated, it seems clear, by alcohol — wrote an editorial for the *Virginia City Territorial Enterprise* charging that funds raised by local women in the name of the Union cause were in fact being sent to "a Miscegenation Society somewhere in the East." Twain later apologized, admitted that the editorial was in poor taste, but at the same time exchanged published insults with the editor of a rival paper, and actually defied his antagonist to meet him in a duel. When push finally came to shove, however, he abruptly left the territory rather than make good on his challenge. Years later, in his *Autobiography*, Twain recast the episode as a comedy in which he is spared the wages of his youthful indiscretions by the rival editor's craven refusal to fight. In Virginia City, personal uncertainty in a framework of sectional divisions led to a trial of manhood in which initial confidence gave way to shameful retreat; but in a manner clearly reminiscent of "The Private History," this apparent failure of nerve was later reconstructed as a comedy of youthful innocence in which all anger and humiliation are laughed away.

Mark Twain came back to his Civil War experiences, as he did to the conflict in Nevada, at a safe remove in time. It was not until 1877, in a speech at a dinner for the Ancient and Honorable Artillery Company of Massachusetts, that he began to compose his memories of the campaign that failed. He recalled in broadly humorous terms, and without reference to bloodshed, that his callow Confederate brigade played at soldiering for a while, and then "disbanded itself and tramped off home, with me" — he added, rather tellingly — "at the tail of it." The success of the speech no doubt figured in the decision, taken eight years later, to cast "The Private History" in a similarly comedic mold. That decision took shape at the bidding of Robert Underwood Johnson, a prominent editor, who urged him to submit an account of his military experiences to the very popular Battles and Leaders of the Civil War series currently featured in *Century* magazine. The piece was several months in the making, and seems to have provoked second thoughts about the wisdom of appearing in print alongside bona fide military heroes of campaigns that had actually succeeded. But Johnson was reassuring. "We shall be glad to see the Missouri sketch," he wrote, "as soon as your timidity as a tyro will admit of your sending it." Months later, when the manuscript finally arrived at the *Century* offices, the editor's confidence was amply rewarded. "The 'Private History' is excellent — 'roarious,'" he rejoiced, no doubt to its author's relief.

Toward the end of his narrative, Twain mentions that in his abortive campaign he barely avoided an armed encounter with Ulysses S. Grant, then an obscure colonel in the advancing Union army. In fact, the paths of the postwar giants never came close to crossing. But the idea of a set-to with the most celebrated of Civil War heroes fascinated Twain, who gravitated to imaginary scenarios in which he achieved moral parity with his wartime opposite, a man of humble origins who conquered fear and rose to the apogee of fame and glory. Here, then, we glimpse another face of the ambiguity which pervades the humorist's treatment of his brief career as a soldier. For even as he joined his countrymen in worshiping the general and former president, he felt the sting of an accusation in the great man's towering example. Twain's esteem for Grant, and his tendency to identify with him, were mingled, as Justin Kaplan has shown, with countering impulses to diminish his lustrous preeminence, and even to destroy him. Such extremes of feeling were no doubt at play in 1885, when Twain oversaw the completion of the dying hero's *Memoirs*. Can we doubt that he experienced a complex inward sense of triumph and vindication as he helped to nurse the failing general through the final stages of the writing, surveyed the enormous profits that the venture would yield to Webster and Company, and delivered to the stricken hero's wife an advance on royalties of $200,000? Working at the same time on "The Private History," and caught up, as Kaplan observes, with the fantasy of facing his friend and nemesis in battle, he tentatively entitled the article "My Campaign Against Grant."

Though critics have differed somewhat in matters of detail, there is little dissent from the view that "The Private History" is a complex and at key points a fictionalized reckoning with a painful chapter from the writer's past. Clearly enough, Mark Twain was not at ease with what he remembered of his Civil War campaign. Nearly as clear is his imperfect success in the sketch at laying those memories to rest. This vexed episode, like so many others that haunted his consciousness, had not finished with him yet. James M. Cox's treatment of "The Private History" stands out precisely because it so effectively integrates the text, and the events which it records, into this longer view of Mark Twain's life and work. Cox observes that until 1885 the Civil War stood out as a conspicuously neglected chapter in Twain's published reconstruction of his personal history. He had written copiously about his boyhood, his years as a Mississippi pilot, his travels both east and west, and his adult experience of the Gilded Age. Indeed, the more he patched the pieces of the past together, the more the gap in the record stood out. But the war "had been not simply forgotten," Cox insists; rather it had been "evaded — and evaded from the very beginning." Samuel Langhorne Clemens adopted the name "Mark Twain" in the Nevada Territory less than two years after his arrival in the mining regions of the Far West. In putting on his new identity, the young man was also groping for a way of escaping the humiliating failure that lay behind him in wartime Missouri. In effect, Cox argues, "the humorous identity and personality of 'Mark Twain' was a grand evasion of the Civil War." Viewed in this comprehensive critical and biographical framework, "The Private History of a Campaign That Failed" forms an important stage in our most popular canonical writer's lifelong — and never completed — project in self-creation.

I am grateful for generous assistance on this essay from Robert H. Hirst, editor of the Mark Twain Papers, and his associates Lin Salamo and Kenneth M. Sanderson.

FOR FURTHER READING

Forrest G. Robinson

Background materials and useful critical discussions of "The Private History of a Campaign That Failed" may be found in James M. Cox, *Mark Twain: The Fate of Humor* (Princeton: Princeton University Press, 1966); Steve Davis, "Mark Twain, the War, and *Life on the Mississippi*," *Southern Studies* 18 (1979), 231–39; John Gerber, "Mark Twain's 'Private Campaign,'" *Civil War History* 1 (1955), 37–60; Justin Kaplan, *Mr. Clemens and Mark Twain* (New York: Simon and Schuster, 1966); Fred W. Lorch, "Mark Twain and the 'Campaign That Failed,'" *American Literature* 12 (1941), 454–70; J. Stanley Mattson, "Mark Twain on War and Peace: The Missouri Rebel and 'The Campaign That Failed,'" *American Quarterly* 20 (1968), 783–94; and Richard E. Peck, "The Campaign that . . . Succeeded," *American Literary Realism* 21 (1989), 3–12. On "The Invalid's Story," see Steven E. Kemper, "Poe, Twain, and Limburger Cheese," *Mark Twain Journal* 21 (1981), 13–14. For a full treatment of the dueling episode in Virginia City, see Paul Fatout, *Mark Twain in Virginia City* (Bloomington: Indiana University Press, 1964), pp. 196–213.

A NOTE ON THE TEXT

Robert H. Hirst

This text of *Merry Tales* is a photographic facsimile of a copy of the first American edition dated 1892 on the title page. The first edition was published early in April 1892; two copies were deposited with the Copyright Office on March 28. All known copies are dated 1892 on the title page, at least in part because the plates were assets of Charles L. Webster and Company, which declared bankruptcy on April 18, 1894. In 1897 the contents of *Merry Tales* (except for "The Invalid's Story" and "The Captain's Story") were collected in *The American Claimant and Other Stories and Sketches,* published by Harper and Brothers as part of a "Uniform Edition." The copy of *Merry Tales* reproduced here is an example of Jacob Blanck's state A: it has decorated endpapers, and it lacks the inserted portrait frontispiece of later states (*BAL* 3435). The deposit copies are also state A, which is therefore likely to be an early impression. The original volume is in the collection of the Mark Twain House in Hartford, Connecticut (810/C625mer/1892/c. 1).

The Mark Twain House is a museum and research center dedicated to the study of Mark Twain, his works, and his times. The museum is located in the nineteen-room mansion in Hartford, Connecticut, built for and lived in by Samuel L. Clemens, his wife, and their three children, from 1874 to 1891. The Picturesque Gothic-style residence, with interior design by the firm of Louis Comfort Tiffany and Associated Artists, is one of the premier examples of domestic Victorian architecture in America. Clemens wrote *Adventures of Huckleberry Finn*, *The Adventures of Tom Sawyer*, *A Connecticut Yankee in King Arthur's Court*, *The Prince and the Pauper*, and *Life on the Mississippi* while living in Hartford.

The Mark Twain House is open year-round. In addition to tours of the house, the educational programs of the Mark Twain House include symposia, lectures, and teacher training seminars that focus on the contemporary relevance of Twain's legacy. Past programs have featured discussions of literary censorship with playwright Arthur Miller and writer William Styron; of the power of language with journalist Clarence Page, comedian Dick Gregory, and writer Gloria Naylor; and of the challenges of teaching *Adventures of Huckleberry Finn* amidst charges of racism.

Anne Bernays is the author of eight novels, among them the award-winning *Growing Up Rich* (1975) and *Professor Romeo* (1989), a *New York Times* Notable Book of the Year. With Pamela Painter, she is the co-author of *What If?* (1990; 1994), a book of writing exercises for fiction writers. She has published short stories, poems, essays, travel pieces, and book reviews in many national magazines and journals, and with her husband, Justin Kaplan, is co-author of a nonfiction book, *The Language of Names*, to be published in Spring 1997. A teacher of fiction writing at Harvard, Boston College and elsewhere since 1975, she occupied the Jenks Chair in Contemporary Letters at the College of the Holy Cross for three years. She lives in Cambridge, Massachusetts.

Shelley Fisher Fishkin, professor of American Studies and English at the University of Texas at Austin, is the author of the award-winning books *Was Huck Black? Mark Twain and African-American Voices* (1993) and *From Fact to Fiction: Journalism and Imaginative Writing in America* (1985). Her most recent book is *Lighting Out for the Territory: Reflections on Mark Twain and American Culture* (1996). She holds a Ph.D. in American Studies from Yale University, has lectured on Mark Twain in Belgium, England, France, Israel, Italy, Mexico, the Netherlands, and Turkey, as well as throughout the United States, and is president-elect of the Mark Twain Circle of America.

Robert H. Hirst is the General Editor of the Mark Twain Project at The Bancroft Library, University of California in Berkeley. Apart from that, he has no other known eccentricities.

Forrest G. Robinson is professor of American Studies at the University of California at Santa Cruz. His books include *The Shape of Things Known: Sidney's Apology in Its Philosophical Tradition* (1972), *Wallace Stegner* (1977), *In Bad Faith: The Dynamics of Deception in Mark Twain's America* (1986), *Love's Story Told: A Life of Henry A. Murray* (1992), and *Having It*

Both Ways: Self-Subversion in Western Popular Classics (1993). He is the editor of *The Cambridge Companion to Mark Twain* (1995), and the co-editor, with Susan Gillman, of *Mark Twain's "Pudd'nhead Wilson": Race, Conflict and Culture* (1990).

ACKNOWLEDGMENTS

There are a number of people without whom The Oxford Mark Twain would not have happened. I am indebted to Laura Brown, senior vice president and trade publisher, Oxford University Press, for suggesting that I edit an "Oxford Mark Twain," and for being so enthusiastic when I proposed that it take the present form. Her guidance and vision have informed the entire undertaking.

Crucial as well, from the earliest to the final stages, was the help of John Boyer, executive director of the Mark Twain House, who recognized the importance of the project and gave it his wholehearted support.

My father, Milton Fisher, believed in this project from the start and helped nurture it every step of the way, as did my stepmother, Carol Plaine Fisher. Their encouragement and support made it all possible. The memory of my mother, Renée B. Fisher, sustained me throughout.

I am enormously grateful to all the contributors to The Oxford Mark Twain for the effort they put into their essays, and for having been such fine, collegial collaborators. Each came through, just as I'd hoped, with fresh insights and lively prose. It was a privilege and a pleasure to work with them, and I value the friendships that we forged in the process.

In addition to writing his fine afterword, Louis J. Budd provided invaluable advice and support, even going so far as to read each of the essays for accuracy. All of us involved in this project are greatly in his debt. Both his knowledge of Mark Twain's work and his generosity as a colleague are legendary and unsurpassed.

Elizabeth Maguire's commitment to The Oxford Mark Twain during her time as senior editor at Oxford was exemplary. When the project proved to be more ambitious and complicated than any of us had expected, Liz helped make it not only manageable, but fun. Assistant editor Elda Rotor's wonderful help in coordinating all aspects of The Oxford Mark Twain, along with literature editor T. Susan Chang's enthusiastic involvement with the project in its final stages, helped bring it all to fruition.

I am extremely grateful to Joy Johannessen for her astute and sensitive copyediting, and for having been such a pleasure to work with. And I appreciate the conscientiousness and good humor with which Kathy Kuhtz Campbell heroically supervised all aspects of the set's production. Oxford president Edward Barry, vice president and editorial director Helen McInnis, marketing director Amy Roberts, publicity director Susan Rotermund, art director David Tran, trade editorial, design and production manager Adam Bohannon, trade advertising and promotion manager Woody Gilmartin, director of manufacturing Benjamin Lee, and the entire staff at Oxford were as supportive a team as any editor could desire.

The staff of the Mark Twain House provided superb assistance as well. I would like to thank Marianne Curling, curator, Debra Petke, education director, Beverly Zell, curator of photography, Britt Gustafson, assistant director of education, Beth Ann McPherson, assistant curator, and Pam Collins, administrative assistant, for all their generous help, and for allowing us to reproduce books and photographs from the Mark Twain House collection. One could not ask for more congenial or helpful partners in publishing.

G. Thomas Tanselle, vice president of the John Simon Guggenheim Memorial Foundation, and an expert on the history of the book, offered essential advice about how to create as responsible a facsimile edition as possible. I appreciate his very knowledgeable counsel.

I am deeply indebted to Robert H. Hirst, general editor of the Mark Twain Project at The Bancroft Library in Berkeley, for bringing his outstanding knowledge of Twain editions to bear on the selection of the books photographed for the facsimiles, for giving generous assistance all along the way, and for providing his meticulous notes on the text. The set is the richer for his advice. I would also like to express my gratitude to the Mark Twain Project, not only for making texts and photographs from their collection available to us, but also for nurturing Mark Twain studies with a steady infusion of matchless, important publications.

I would like to thank Jeffrey Kaimowitz, curator of the Watkinson Library at Trinity College, Hartford (where the Mark Twain House collection is kept), along with his colleagues Peter Knapp and Alesandra M. Schmidt, for having been instrumental in Robert Hirst's search for first editions that could be safely reproduced. Victor Fischer, Harriet Elinor Smith, and especially Kenneth M. Sanderson, associate editors with the Mark Twain Project, reviewed the note on the text in each volume with cheerful vigilance. Thanks are also due to Mark Twain Project associate editor Michael Frank and administrative assistant Brenda J. Bailey for their help at various stages.

I am grateful to Helen K. Copley for granting permission to publish photographs in the Mark Twain Collection of the James S. Copley Library in La Jolla, California, and to Carol Beales and Ron Vanderhye of the Copley Library for making my research trip to their institution so productive and enjoyable.

Several contributors — David Bradley, Louis J. Budd, Beverly R. David, Robert Hirst, Fred Kaplan, James S. Leonard, Toni Morrison, Lillian S. Robinson, Jeffrey Rubin-Dorsky, Ray Sapirstein, and David L. Smith — were particularly helpful in the early stages of the project, brainstorming about the cast of writers and scholars who could make it work. Others who participated in that process were John Boyer, James Cox, Robert Crunden, Joel Dinerstein, William Goetzmann, Calvin and Maria Johnson, Jim Magnuson, Arnold Rampersad, Siva Vaidhyanathan, Steve and Louise Weinberg, and Richard Yarborough.

Kevin Bochynski, famous among Twain scholars as an "angel" who is gifted at finding methods of making their research run more smoothly, was helpful in more ways than I can count. He did an outstanding job in his official capacity as production consultant to The Oxford Mark Twain, supervising the photography of the facsimiles. I am also grateful to him for having put me in touch via e-mail with Kent Rasmussen, author of the magisterial *Mark Twain A to Z*, who was tremendously helpful as the project proceeded, sharing insights on obscure illustrators and other points, and generously being "on call" for all sorts of unforeseen contingencies.

I am indebted to Siva Vaidhyanathan of the American Studies Program of the University of Texas at Austin for having been such a superb research assistant. It would be hard to imagine The Oxford Mark Twain without the benefit of his insights and energy. A fine scholar and writer in his own right, he was crucial to making this project happen.

Georgia Barnhill, the Andrew W. Mellon Curator of Graphic Arts at the American Antiquarian Society in Worcester, Massachusetts, Tom Staley, director of the Harry Ransom Humanities Research Center at the University of Texas at Austin, and Joan Grant, director of collection services at the Elmer Holmes Bobst Library of New York University, granted us access to their collections and assisted us in the reproduction of several volumes of The Oxford Mark Twain. I would also like to thank Kenneth Craven, Sally Leach, and Richard Oram of the Harry Ransom Humanities Research Center for their help in making HRC materials available, and Jay and John Crowley, of Jay's Publishers Services in Rockland, Massachusetts, for their efforts to photograph the books carefully and attentively.

I would like to express my gratitude for the grant I was awarded by the University Research Institute of the University of Texas at Austin to defray some of the costs of researching The Oxford Mark Twain. I am also grateful to American Studies director Robert Abzug and the University of Texas for the computer that facilitated my work on this project (and to UT systems analyst Steve Alemán, who tried his best to repair the damage when it crashed). Thanks also to American Studies administrative assistant Janice Bradley and graduate coordinator Melanie Livingston for their always generous and thoughtful help.

The Oxford Mark Twain would not have happened without the unstinting, wholehearted support of my husband, Jim Fishkin, who went way beyond the proverbial call of duty more times than I'm sure he cares to remember as he shared me unselfishly with that other man in my life, Mark Twain. I am also grateful to my family — to my sons Joey and Bobby, who cheered me on all along the way, as did Fannie Fishkin, David Fishkin, Gennie Gordon, Mildred Hope Witkin, and Leonard, Gillis, and Moss

Plaine — and to honorary family member Margaret Osborne, who did the same.

My greatest debt is to the man who set all this in motion. Only a figure as rich and complicated as Mark Twain could have sustained such energy and interest on the part of so many people for so long. Never boring, never dull, Mark Twain repays our attention again and again and again. It is a privilege to be able to honor his memory with The Oxford Mark Twain.

Shelley Fisher Fishkin
Austin, Texas
April 1996